ROACH

First Published in Great Britain 2015 by Mirador Publishing

Copyright © 2015 by Alisa Perederey

Cover image © 2015 Heidy Gomez Lazarovsky, HG2 Media

First edition: 2015

Any reference to real names and places are purely fictional and are constructs of the author. Any offence the references produce is unintentional and in no way reflects the reality of any locations or people involved.

A copy of this work is available through the British Library.

ISBN: 978-1-911044-18-5

Mirador Publishing
Mirador
Wearne Lane
Langport
Somerset
TA10 9HB

ROACH

By

Alisa Perederey

No matter how the story ends, always remember how it all began.

PART ONE

Chapter 1

He can smell the morning as it came. The sun had borne a hole through his curtains as he slowly got up from bed. It was the exact same morning as every morning prior. Same routine; nothing ever changes, not anymore.

It's been a while since the New York nightlife had a gig. Depressing are the all too quiet nights in a place that used to be called "the city that never sleeps." Now, no one ever goes out, not anymore. Not that there are too many inhabitants left in the once overcrowded metropolis. The ones that did remain, however, almost had no choice. Griffin Scoarse was one of the unlucky ones.

He made his usual cup of coffee and got dressed for work. He dreaded having to go into that factory but he did it day after day. He used to listen to music on his walk to work but now it seemed to have lost its appeal. He walked in pure silence not bothering to dodge the trash spewed across the sidewalks. Old newspapers usually, sometimes some rancid uneaten meals were paired with the insects that accompanied them. Before, he would make an effort to walk to the beat of the music as he stepped across the garbage and avoided the chemical spoilage that now covered the streets. As time went on, no one bothered to clean up the mess. Now, there was no point to avoid it. He stomped on it, along it, dealing with the stench and exhaustion of the mildew. He was now a part of that mess and fully accepted his role within it.

Weapons. That was his job. His only use was to press a simple button on the conveyor belt, making sure each pistol was made efficiently and with no faults. He used to get so weary of it all. *This pointless job that any moron can do.* It took him some time to finally accept that he was *that* moron. From nine to five he would sit on his stool watching the guns rotate along the assembly line, take a coffee break once or twice a day; eat the same gray meal they dared to call food at the cafeteria.

He should have felt productive in a way, maybe even accomplished at the end of each day as he slowly slipped into the same pajamas before heading off to bed. However, his mind would begin to race with thoughts that could have easily thrown anyone into so deep a depression—a numbing depression that would inevitably cause the thought of a blade going down their wrist seem like the most beautifully intoxicating sense of peace that could ever come across any man. Though the thought of suicide seemed so tempting; Griffin Scoarse would never be capable of ceasing to care. And care about what exactly? He never did know. What he was certain of though, was the sense of hope that had accompanied him throughout his entire life. That small little glimmer of hope—that somehow, in some way, his life would be worth it. That one day, it will all change. One day, he will be able to wake up in the morning and look forward to the day that was yet to come. One day, Griffin Scoarse will be proud of who he was as he stared into his own eyes while brushing his teeth at the bathroom sink. Instead, all he saw now was a man not worthy of the oxygen that now entered his lungs.

It had been a long day at the factory; something he'd already come to expect. And, just like any day he couldn't wait to race out of the building as soon as his shift was over. He sat by the just assembled pistols staring at the hands of the clock on the wall waiting for 5 pm to strike. As soon as his workday was over he'd hurry outside to the cold breeze of the New York City streets and light up his cigarette. For a man who had no plans after work, he amazed even himself at his own sense of urgency to get out of that building.

He slowly inhaled his cigarette pretending to enjoy the only thing that he so desperately wanted to believe brought him some type of pleasure. He hated the routine of everyday life but followed his own custom of stubbing out his half smoked Marlboro Light as he walked across the street to the only deli that remained open and bought his third cup of coffee for the day. He lit up another cigarette as he began his walk home.

It would have been just like any other day if it hadn't been for her. He should have sensed it in the cold chill that ran down his spine when he saw her head of golden waves crossing the street toward him. Of course it was unusual for anyone, especially a gorgeous young female to be walking the streets of New York. However, it hadn't fazed him enough to pay any attention to what anyone else would have known as something so completely out of the ordinary. He only noticed her and nothing else. It was hard not to think about her and to disregard everything else when she had approached him. He was confused but most of all he was curious. *Who was she and why was she walking toward him?* He seemed to forget that no one else was around for at least another few blocks.

She smiled as she approached him. A smile that would have instantly lit up any room. The type where everyone noticed her and wanted to know who she was. Except this time, Griffin was the only one around to see it. The only soul with the fortunate luck to have witnessed such beauty in so dark a world.

Her eyes on the other hand told a different story. As she came closer he saw the sadness and fear behind those big green daggers of hers. That's when it all hit him; she shouldn't be here, rather, she couldn't possibly be here. Wherever she came from, there must be a number of authorities searching for her. He suddenly felt that same chill from before and took it as a warning. He began to turn his back on her when she suddenly spoke. "Please, don't walk away from me. I need your help."

Chapter 2

"Griffin when are you going to wake up and smell the coffee?" The phrase often lurks in the back of his head, almost like a bad dream; every time he thinks of his deceased mother.

He had been nineteen years old back when his mother had woken him up in the afternoon by asking the question. He had responded in a sarcastic; and hostile manner, which now fuels his long regret diary. Upon having heard the saying escape his mother's lips he had chosen to mock her by taking it far too literally. After rolling out of bed about half an hour later he'd gone into the kitchen and poured a cup of coffee from the freshly brewed carafe awaiting him. "Mmmm" he said when he inhaled the aroma given off by the coffee as he purposely mimicked the old nineties *Folgers* commercial. "Reminds me of the morning and the fresh new day ahead" he continued to describe the scent of the caffeine he now held in his right hand, in his favorite mug at the time. It was a big white mug with black polka dots decorated all around it. The design often reminded him of cows, which in his mind, was quite fitting especially when he added a quarter of a cup of milk to his coffee.

Mrs. Scoarse had come into the kitchen by then and watched her son with patience. For the past nineteen years she'd had such hopes for him. She had sacrificed everything to bring him to New York; the city where dreams come true. If her dreams couldn't become a reality she had been bent on making sure her son's did. As the years went by she began to realize just how little dreaming Griffin actually did.

He had decided not to go to class that day. That wasn't unusual in his case. Back in high school he rarely attended classes, so rare in fact that the school threatened to postpone his graduation. He didn't care much at the time whether or not he did get his diploma. However, the look of sorrow and devastation on his mother's face after hearing the news caused him to go back and do whatever was necessary to graduate on time. With Griffin Scoarse this meant lie as much as possible. He'd concocted such a story of being ill and depressed that the teachers took pity on him and gave him passing marks. To make his mother happy he attended college the following year. Yet, old habits die hard.

It's not that the courses were difficult. On the contrary, it had all been too simple for him. This simplicity was the reason he stopped coming to class on a regular basis. He was proud to proclaim himself "self-taught" when his peers would often remark on his lack attendance that coupled with his amazing grades. Soon enough he would stop studying all together. He'd later remark that he would just "wing it" on the exams; but his grades had dropped. Not drastically of course; just from an A to a B but a drop nonetheless. He was not as perfect as he believed himself to be. This did not encourage him to start attending classes; instead he came up with more elaborate lies to tell his professors. The more they pitied him the less he would worry about his studies.

At the age of nineteen he was in his junior year of college and still felt like a freshman when he entered the school. He would have given up all together and dropped out if it hadn't been for his mother. He couldn't bear to see her expression if he'd told her he wanted to drop out. But this arrangement made him extremely unhappy. He had gone on for a long time believing that his lacking attendance was the cause of his depression. That he wasted his days and that was the reason for his feeling unproductive every night. However, nothing changed. Not his attendance, not his mood, and most importantly, not his lack of ambition.

He drank his coffee that afternoon with a cigarette in between his fingers. His mother had turned on the television to watch the news. It was the same story as before; warnings of war. They were not urgent warnings; no one believed that war would be imminent. The news simply claimed that due to the threat of nuclear weapons the United States must be on guard. If worst came to worst all they would have to face was a quick war with all of Western Europe on their side. It all seemed like a joke.

Bored with the same stories, his mother got up to do the dishes in the sink. She gestured for him to take out the garbage. Ignoring her he turned his back. "Please, don't walk away from me. I need your help." Those would be the last words he would ever hear his mother say. He continued to ignore her as he walked back into his room, locked the door, pulled down his pajamas and turned on his computer.

That had been twenty years ago.

Chapter 3

He sat there staring at her for what seemed like hours. He hadn't asked her who she was and she never told him. They chose to remain as strangers. It had been a mutual agreement; no words were necessary.

Upon bringing her to his apartment he made them both a warm cup of tea. She held her cup in both hands desperately trying to absorb all the heat. Her hands were trembling and her legs shaking. He knew it wasn't from the cold. He could sense how she felt. The cold came from deep inside of her. Whatever happened to her, whatever it was that brought her to this point, had clearly shaken her. He knew she would never forget.

After sipping their tea in silence she finally spoke "I want to take a ride. Just get in that car, blast my music, drive and just feel...I just want to feel. Feel with no consequences."

She paused then. Looking over at Griffin she smiled, grateful that he let her speak.

"If I had told everyone that I love just how much they mean to me would anything have even changed? Or would we still be lost...so broken... What is that purpose that we're all looking for? What is it that I'm looking for? What is the price for my happiness, our happiness? I pray for strength, I just don't know who or what it is that I'm praying to. Can anyone even hear my prayers? Its nights like these where I feel more alone than I've ever imagined. Is this what I want? It all kills me."

She wasn't speaking to him. Her thoughts were simply for her own benefit. A way to clear her mind, a way to vent. A simple way to deal with reality. He felt her pain, he shared it with her. They were no different, not anymore. Maybe, years ago, when they were young, neither of them would have ever imagined meeting the other. They each had their own separate lives. But now, how everything had turned out; not just for them but for the entire world, there wasn't much that could differentiate them.

"Do you smoke?" He asked casually. He needed something to alleviate the tension.

She responded with a nod. He took that as his cue and opened the small drawer on his bedside table. He pulled out some marijuana along with his blue and white-spiraled bowl. He packed it carefully before taking his first hit of the night. The lighter fumbled in his hand as he went to pass the weed.

Drugs weren't hard to find. He had yet to meet anyone who didn't smoke nowadays. The drug cartels were booming with business since the war while the rest of the world economy was crashing. Most people had turned to drugs, including alcohol, as a means to escape reality. Dope and meth were everywhere but he preferred marijuana. It used to help him sleep at night now he smoked out of habit. A few times a month he would drop an E pill and enter an entirely new world. He looked forward to the ecstasy but the little that remained of his self-control stopped him from turning it into a regular activity. Marijuana allowed him to cope in the meantime.

After a half hour they had smoked two bowls and were feeling its effects. In the past they would have been giggling by now but not even weed could make them forget. Instead they got sat in silence as he turned on the television. There wasn't much on which came as no surprise. He decided on the news and left that on making sure to lower the volume to just white noise.

He continued to watch her as she stared at the TV. The images meant nothing to her as she mellowed out and slowly began to close her eyes. He felt burnt as well but couldn't look away. She reminded him of someone from his past and thought of her as an angel. She definitely looked like one. He made sure not to make any advances on her because he felt it would spoil his perception of what he saw her as; innocence. But now with her eyes closed he couldn't ignore her body. She was a woman after all and it had been a long time since he felt the touch of one. He watched her breasts move up and down as she slowly inhaled. He focused on her legs which seemed to go on for miles underneath her dark denim jeans. He observed her lips and wondered what it would be like to kiss them.

He began to feel a strong trembling in between his legs. He longed to touch her but his morals got the best of him. She'd asked him for help and she trusted him. He did not want to abuse that trust. Instead he gently woke her and walked her to his bed. He helped her get out of her boots and slipped the comforter over her. As he turned towards the bathroom she mutely whispered a thank you. Those two small words suddenly meant the world to him as he began to form a minute smile.

In that moment he couldn't help but sit at the foot of the bed and continue to look over her. He packed a third bowl himself and smoked it in silence, all the while paying attention to the sleeping stranger in his bed. It took whatever strength he had left in him to get up, put on his jacket and go outside.

Once outside he lit up a cigarette. He checked his pockets for whatever bills he had and counted them up. He had enough. He walked two blocks to the destination where he knew they'd be waiting. He had made it a point in the past to never indulge in such sin but he could not help himself. He'd only paid for sex twice before and on those rare occasions he had been desperate. Tonight he needed to get rid of his urges. It was the only solution he was able to think of that would help him control his thirst.

Chapter 4

He woke up the next morning with a pounding headache and an itchy crotch. He sat at the couch clutching his pillow for a half hour trying to figure out what had happened the previous night. Through his half open bedroom door he could see her sound asleep and decided not to wake her as he got up and went into the shower. He scrubbed with all the strength he could muster trying to get the stink off of him. When he dried off and got dressed he still felt dirty.

To get his mind away from the thought of regret he smoked a bowl while the coffee was brewing. He made sure to make enough for two. Before leaving for the factory he smoked a cigarette with his coffee and left her a note by the bed stand explaining that he will be back in the evening. He did not expect her to stay and wait for him. He knew she needed a place to stay last night and that was it. Though all logic told him that it would be best if she disappeared and he forgot all about her, he still hoped she'd be there when he returned.

He could not stop thinking about her. All day at work he'd look towards the exit with anticipation thinking she'd walk through the doors at any moment carrying a brown bag of lunch for him. He wanted a turkey and Swiss cheese sandwich. A part of him believed this delusion. It helped him get through the workday quicker, but as the clock neared 5 pm he'd begun to lose hope. Suddenly, a flood of disappointment washed over him. He did not want to admit to himself that it was quite unlikely that she'd still be in his apartment.

He walked home filled with despair and uneasiness. He

wanted so desperately for her to be there but knew not to expect it. He knew how let down he would feel if he were to discover her gone. He prepared himself for the worst as he stuck his key into the lock.

He walked in to an empty apartment. There was no proof that she'd even been there. The remainder of the coffee from that morning was untouched, his bed was made, the note was nowhere to be seen, and she was gone. It took him sometime to accept this. He checked every corner of his apartment to make sure. He went so far as to look behind the shower curtain. Upon finally facing the reality of her departure he went outside. He walked back towards the factory to the deli. He got himself a turkey sandwich and walked towards one of the benches stationed outside the factory.

He sat down and rolled off the foil to reveal the sandwich. He took a bite. It tasted horrible. He quickly spat it out and to no one in particular announced that the sandwich tasted like complete shit. For six dollars he was expecting a decent turkey sandwich. He stared down at the gray turkey underneath the bread and suddenly felt bad for himself. He'd paid for it. He took another bite and this time he swallowed it.

He began to think back to when he was in high school. His mother would always pack him his lunch in a brown bag. Every day, Monday through Friday, it had been the same thing; a turkey and Swiss cheese sandwich. She used to leave for work before school started so she rarely ever knew if he'd be attending class that day. Sometimes he'd eat the sandwich when his munches struck him. However, on most days, he'd forget all about the sandwich and by evening it'd go bad. Sometimes he would dispose of it and tell her later that evening how appetizing his lunch was when she'd come back from work. Other days she'd throw the sandwich out herself never saying a word about it. Either way, she always knew when the sandwich had been wasted. Yet, day after day she continued to make him his lunch.

He suddenly felt sick. He looked down yet again at the sandwich in his hand and rolled it back up. He got up from the bench and went home, sandwich in hand.

Before entering his building he took another long look at his sandwich. He could feel the screams building up inside of him. He could feel them getting caught in his throat. He lost control and crushed whatever was left of the turkey and cheese and threw it onto the pavement that would become its new home before a rat came along. The screams were only getting stronger, building up inside his throat and chest. His headache started to come back along with the self-disgust that he'd felt that morning. He kneeled against the light pole on the corner and began to vomit.

It was only when he'd spewed chunks all over them that he noticed the black boots standing by his side.

Chapter 5

For years we've gone – as simple gatherers, no matter how hard we deny it. Day after day we slave for society. We wake up in the morning; go about our daily routines never paying much mind to why it is that we do what we do. We come home during the evening and finally go to bed at night. We've forgotten how to dream. We seem to have lost our ability to question everything and everyone. We simply accept things as the way they are and never think twice about anything. However, it has come down to this very point, this very moment. We shall soon cease to exist, at least, in our definition of existence itself.

Those were the opening words to the pamphlet of hope; the pamphlet that would have changed the future if anyone had paid any attention to it. Griffin folded it up and stuck it in his back pocket and forgot all about it. He did not care much for the rebels or the rebellion they were so adamant on enforcing. He swiped his monthly-unlimited metro card at the subway station and waited for the train. Instead of looking back at the pamphlet and killing time with the words of what should have been the next revolution he took out his iPod and blasted his music to drown out the sounds of the underground city.

He was on his way to his mother's funeral and by the looks of it, he was running late. His grief had yet to hit him as he was still in a constant state of denial. However, he did recall the afternoon when he had last seen his mother; only three days ago. She had left work and he hadn't even bothered to leave his room to say good-bye. She had yelled a good bye to him before closing the front door behind her; at the time he'd paid no attention.

On that unfortunate evening, on her way back home from the city, she just happened to be at the wrong place at the wrong time. It had been quite a few years after 9/11 thus no one expected it to ever happen again. Of course, ignorance had been the fog. This was New York City after all, and with all the enemies the United States had made over the years Americans should have been more prepared. With the threat of nuclear warfare it came as no surprise to government officials that the city had suffered a bombing. For a few years they referred to it as yet another terrorist attack, however, the world should have known better.

Her body had not been found under all the rubble and it was for this reason alone that Griffin chose to remain in a state of denial. *He* should have known better.

At the memorial service he received the usual redundant banal condolences from relatives he never knew he had and family friends he'd never met. They all made him sick. He began to wonder where the hell they all had been when his mother had needed financial help, when she had needed a shoulder to cry on, when she had needed someone to comfort her about her good for nothing son. Instead, he simply thanked each and every one of them for having shown up with their empty pity.

While staring at his mother's photograph surrounded with flowers he suddenly felt very grateful that they had not been able to find her body. He couldn't bear the thought of having to see her lowered down into the cold dark ground in a casket in a cemetery. He hadn't allowed himself to think of where her body could actually be in that moment, and in what horrendous disfigured, mutilated condition she was in.

There was no wake. He'd made sure of that. He'd gone back home and entered his mother's room. He sat on her bed for a long time trying to rationalize what had happened, trying to accept the fact that she was gone and was never going to come back. He sat there staring at the green carpet searching for any sign of her. He could faintly smell her favorite perfume coating her bedroom, a marriage of lavender and minute notes of vanilla. He noticed a picture of him at the age of seven in grade school by her bed stand. He still was unable to fully realize what had truly occurred. He continued to hope that at any moment she would walk in through the front door just as she had always done after work and quietly complain about the sink full of dishes as she got busy preparing dinner. But she never did come through that door. The dishes still remained unwashed and the fridge was full of rotting unprepared produce.

He stared at his picture once more realizing that she had woken up every morning to that portrait when her alarm had gone off at 7 AM and went to sleep to it every night. He felt the tears beginning to form. His vision got hazy as he began to sob. He couldn't hold it in any longer. Denial was no longer a means of escape as acceptance began to flow through his veins. His tears continued to roll down no matter how hard he tried to stop. Every time he looked around her bedroom he was reminded of her memory, of her strength, of her love for him and his regret. He hated himself more than anything in that moment. He felt the sickness coming up and ran to the bathroom.

He sat there by the toilet covered in his vomit and drenched in tears. It was too late to make amends. It was too late to make her happy. It was too late to tell her that he would make her proud. He can no longer embrace her and tell her how much he loved her. How much she had meant to him. It all seemed so cliché; now that she was dead did he finally came to terms with just how much he had taken her for granted. He felt alone, lost, and so broken. He would have given anything to go back and change who he was, change who he had become. But it was far too late for any of that. He would struggle for the rest of his life trying to come to terms with the man he was; never accepting himself and yet never capable of change.

Chapter 6

"I thought you'd left"

"No, where would I go?" She laughed then. "I'm sorry, I didn't mean it like that"

"So, where did you go?" He asked with confusion.

She stared at him for a long time. He began to feel as if he'd asked the wrong thing. He didn't mean to act like the concerned father and he wasn't in the least bit curious as to where she had been, he was simply confused. *Why would she choose to remain here with him?* Yes, she had no where else to go but she could have kept running, found some place else, found someone else to keep her company.

"We should go inside" was all she said with a sincere smile on her face.

Once inside his apartment she made them both tea and explained that she simply went out for a walk to clear her head. It all seemed innocent enough. He didn't want to pry any further and decided to leave her alone. She had other ideas in mind.

"I need to tell you a few things about myself" she said as she sat down on one of the old, rotten wooden chairs in his closet of a kitchen.

Her story began with her explaining her family history. It came as a surprise for him to learn that she had grown up on a farm in a small town in some western state. She had not disclosed any details such as the names of her hometown or what company her family had been farming for. She did mention that her family specialized in chickens. They had been farmers for generations and had bred many chickens over the decades; in short, they were specialists at what they did. Her ancestors had made a good living with the money they had made from the farm.

From the late nineties to the start of the new millennium her family had begun to experience financial troubles. During that time period, big food industries had begun to grow more powerful as they virtually became monopolies in the industry. She explained that the chicken coups in which the chickens were bred became more and more inhumane as they started to resemble dark torture houses. The chickens were changing as well; they had been ingested with growth hormones, which had caused them to grow quite large in size and weight, so much so that most of the chickens were unable to walk, as they could not carry their own weight.

This was all due to the ever-expanding industry. Large food companies often forced many farmers into contracts that would allow for the industry to grow as the farmer became poorer in the process. Pretty soon her family had stumbled into a heap of debt that would eventually tear them a part. Not wanting to be rid of the family business her father stood his ground in the industry and pretended that everything was all right as her mother could no longer handle their dwindling bank accounts that would inevitably push into the negatives. What was once the perfect family farm soon consisted of four individuals who could no longer stand the sight of one another. Before the war overseas had begun, her family had been fighting a war within themselves for years, unable to muster the strength to defeat what had initially brought them to this point: big food industry.

She had been only thirteen years old when her mother had killed herself. Her older sister had been the one to discover her mother's body in their parents' bedroom. The sight had caused her to become sick before the grief had set in.

Years afterward her father had blamed himself for her suicide and in order to cope with her death and the guilt he'd become an alcoholic. His drunken nights would eventually lead into drunken days during which he was unable to control himself. The sight of his daughters would remind him of his deceased wife and failure as both a husband and a father. Instead of reaching out for help he would lock himself away in the basement for days at a time forgetting the outside world. When he would come out both girls would cower in terror as they fled to a nearby neighbor's home for safety.

After a couple more years of this she was no longer strong enough to maintain the lifestyle and go on pretending that everything was all right. She went into her sister's bedroom and begged her to leave with her; explaining that they can start over some place new and lead a better life. Her frightened sister ignored her, refusing to leave her father alone on the abandoned farm to perish in his waste. On a cold October night, covered in bruises for the last time, a few months before the war had begun the draft, she decided to leave on her own.

After a few days her sister had contacted the local authorities and filled out a missing persons report. However, due to the sky rocketing drug crimes surrounding much of the rural United States, not much of an investigation had been conducted during that time period. Meth had become one of the most dangerous drugs and almost every individual living in rural towns had been invited to the party. The police were far too busy busting up lab after lab and arresting those involved in trafficking the drug to worry too much about a missing person. After only several weeks they simply proclaimed her as dead and the documents, along with her death certificate were written up. From that point on she never contacted her family again and had been on the run ever since, never being able to find a new home due to the war that now ruined much of the country.

She had ended her story there and Griffin just sat there in astonishment, confusion, and pity. He still had many questions for her including what her name was but decided that all of that could wait. After thinking through everything she had told him about the past he calculated that she had been she'd been away from her family for the past seven years. At the same time he felt disgusted with himself; here he was given every opportunity in life and he was still pathetic, whereas she had gone through trauma after trauma and continued to live.

He was suddenly envious of her strength and ability to keep going. He stared down at his hands, and saw that they had neither a scratch nor scar on them. His hands were well kept for the simple reason that he rarely used them for anything. Her hands on the other hand, were covered in cracks as her dry skin continued to erode them. His mother had once told him that in order to discover if an individual works more with their body than their mind, or just works at all, all you need to do is to look at their hands.

"Becks"

"What?" He stared up in confusion, suddenly remembering where he was.

"That's my name; Becks."

Chapter 7

"They will never know
Because they will never be
Don't you understand?
It's us; you and I, how it always was.

Yes! Invoke in them; give it all away.
Providence—we screech.
Our marker already begun to bleed.
The blood of the sun, we will shine one day.

Difference we shall embrace.
Forgiveness we will provide.
Hold up to the lies—the insanity.
The gruesome truth we hide in sarcastic voices…"

"What are you reading?" he asked, entering the apartment.

"The rebels' pamphlet I found it in the back pocket of a pair of old jeans. I hope you don't mind but I cleaned up a bit in here while you were away at work. I was bored and didn't have much else to do."

"I don't mind its fine" He'd already forgotten about the poem.

He stared at the jeans lying on the ground next to her recalling the last time he had worn them; it had been his mother's funeral. He never intended to put them on ever again but never got around to disposing the pair either. At some point he had contemplated on burning them.

He'd associated the pair with his mother's death; he had worn them for a few days after he first received news of the bombing. He was unable to bring himself to change out of them until after the funeral. He remembered wearing them when he was in her bedroom focused on the picture she kept of him on the bed stand. When he had left her bedroom he had finally torn them off of himself and threw them in his closet. He'd simply forgotten all about their existence until now. He noticed that the vomit stains were still visible on the jeans; after all these years the proof of his grief stricken remorse continued to live. He supposed it was a sign of remembrance; to never forget his past mistakes.

She noticed his concentrated expression and knew that his mind had gone elsewhere. She assumed he was thinking back to the days of the revolution; the times when there was still hope instilled in the people before everything had failed. "Were you a part of the revolution?" she asked.

"Huh...what?" He looked up as if noticing her there for the first time.

"Were you one of the rebels of the failed revolution?"

He caught a glimpse of interest in her voice and suddenly became aware of the fact that she really knew nothing about him. He could let her believe that he had been a rebel before his factory days; it would easily make him seem less pathetic if he went along with a lie. Just played pretend, at least for a little while.

"Yes, I was" The lie felt weird coming out of his mouth but he embraced it.

He watched her emerald eyes light up and instantly felt better about it, here was his chance to impress her, to make her believe he was someone worth praising.

"Why don't I make us some tea and I can tell you all about

my rebel days" He already had an entire story mapped out in his mind.

Of course there would be loopholes but he was always good at filling in the gaps especially on the spot. It was simple for him; just build up from one lie and keep going. He was so good at it in fact that a part of him always believed his own lies.

As he told her his story he felt more empowered than he had in a long while. She listened to his every word with wonder and amazement; he was a hero to her now. He was someone who portrayed the utmost courage and confidence; a man who fought for what he believed in, a man who never gave up, not until the bitter end. He was now able to feel that same characterization flow through his veins. He envisioned himself in black rebels' attire attending the marches and speaking at every gathering. He began to feel as if he had truly been an individual with real purpose; a youth with a cause, pride quickly began to seep into his skin.

"Do you remember some of the speeches you used to give?" Becks asked. His lies were so real at this point that he didn't even hesitate as he recited the first thing that came to his head.

"This is the closing line to one of my more popular speeches," He explained before he went on. "It's like I said before; we're all going to kill ourselves one day. We're all walking around with a fucking noose tied around our necks just waiting for that final nudge off the chair. You just wait and see."

Becks leaned in close. "I want to hear your heart beating" she said. "I want to hear your blood pumping through your veins. I want to hear it throb" she leaned in real close…

Chapter 8

The factory will be shutting down soon. They'd announced it during the lunch break. Apparently there were far too many weapons being manufactured and not enough soldiers to use them anymore. That was inevitable. Griffin left work early that evening, no point in abiding to the rules now that he'll be out of a job soon enough. He had no clue as to where he would go next. He should have prepared for this better. They had warned him that the factory wouldn't survive through the entire war but he always thought he'd cross that bridge when he got to it. Well, he got to it, but now he doesn't even know where the bridge begins, let alone attempt to cross it. Once again his legs don't work properly. And again he's reminded of his failed existence.

When the war had first begun he had every intention in doing what was right for his country. Every intention in making his mother proud though she was no longer around to reap the benefits. He would go to sleep well past midnight with every intent to get up before noon and sign up for recruitment. However, waking up at five PM didn't help and he'd never made it to a single recruitment office. Not until the draft.

The draft left him with no excuses. He would have to go and fight, he would have to become someone. He saw it as a sign and though fear still steered his life he'd so desperately wanted to believe that he would finally become a man. That never happened.

He showed up to the recruitment office around three PM on

a sunny May afternoon. His medical exam failed him. They couldn't have a soldier with a failed kidney and liver damage. No, they couldn't have a soldier who suffered from asthma. No, they couldn't have a soldier who was so underweight for his height that he could barely hold a rifle. No, his steadily worsening vision was not good enough. No, they couldn't have a soldier who was unable to pass the psych exam. No, depression and weakness in one's moral wasn't good enough. No, those hallucinations he sometimes experienced wouldn't make the cut. No, those drugs found in his blood stream weren't contributing. They told him he would work in the arms factory. At least he had a job.

Now he no longer had that job. He should have brought home one of the rifles he'd helped make all these years. He should have put it to his right temple and pulled the trigger. He should have done it on the first day at the factory. He hadn't the courage. His delusions often betrayed him. *Why kill myself now when I have yet to leave a mark in this world?* He'd often say to himself. Oh yes, he still believed he was destined for greatness. Still believed he would one day wake up and become someone. Still envisioned people flocking to his side to bring him praise. Still fantasized about becoming one of the greatest and most successful, not to mention most respected men alive. He honestly believed they'd build a statute of gold in his honor, believed that the generations to succeed him would always carry him in their memories until the end of time.

Those same delusions continue to be his enemy. He walked back to the apartment without a clue as to how to proceed now. How he would pay for rent, food, anything at all, was beyond him. It should have destroyed him. He was far from destruction now. His coping mechanism sprung into high gear.

If he concentrated hard enough he'd be able to hear the nuts and bolts in his brain rattling, sending vibrations throughout his body. *Yes, this was meant to happen*, he thought to himself. *Everything happens for a reason.*

What reason would that be? No, logical thought escaped him now. To face reality yet again would only bring on another involuntary purge. That, he couldn't handle right now. Better to hide behind a façade, safer to let his mind run wild with fantasy and delirium. *Only a stepping-stone toward something better.* He entered the apartment.

"I heard about the factory" Becks told him as he slid out of his old boots. "Decided to get you a little pick me up" She held up a little plastic bag. It was coke no doubt about it, looked to be about a gram.

"I've never done blow before; never tried it" He confessed.

"You'll like it. Don't worry, I'll get it set up" She began making lines on the little coffee table in the kitchen.

He watched her with full concentration. She took some of the crystal white powder out of the small Ziploc-like bag and began using a Metrocard to break it up. Her hands moved quickly as she cut the powder thinner and thinner until there was double the amount as before on the table. The crystals were minuscule, refined. "No nosebleeds this way" she explained.

She began breaking up the powdery heap into four lines; four perfectly shaped lines. She rolled up a twenty-dollar bill into a thin tube. She'd definitely done this before. "Two lines each, I'll go first." She put the carefully rolled up twenty dollar tube toward her right nostril and bent down over the table. The bill was slanted as it touched the table and she snorted an entire line in just a second.

He did as she instructed and snorted his line before she

went for her second. It hit his brain in an instant. He smelled the baking soda, it reminded him or horseradish. It was different, but not entirely so. He took his second line without hesitation. He felt the same at first, didn't really know what to do with the sensation. Then she put on some music; the Rolling Stones blasted throughout the apartment. He wanted to move. He liked the movement. He wanted to talk. He liked the talking. He was suddenly more amicable then ever before. He became, in those few seconds, an entirely new person. Getting wired on blow wasn't just an energy boost for him; it was an *everything* boost.

She licked her index finger and picked up the residue off the table and smudged it on to her gums. He did the same, and instantly his gums went numb. The taste itself was wonderful.

"I'm going to change the world Becks!" He shouted over the music. "We're going to be happy, you'll see! Everything's going to work out!" He truly believed it. In that moment, he was invincible.

He was in awe that he'd never tried blow before. Where had it been all his life? He'd done plenty of other drugs in the past. He'd been around cocaine before, seen people do it, but never bothered to try it. He never realized how good it was, never tried to understand how people got so addicted to it before. He knew now. He liked being this new person. Unlike E pills where he got an artificial feeling of euphoria, coke gave him a high that felt entirely natural. It was him; a part of him that he'd never had the balls to let out before. Coke made him in to a new and improved version of his past self. Same old Griffin just friendlier, happier, more energetic. He loved it. Until the comedown.

Becks didn't see it. She didn't understand. Unlike him, she wasn't plagued with an addictive personality. Nothing felt right in that moment. He didn't know what to do with himself. She noticed him withdrawing back into himself. He was no longer moving to the music. He'd stopped conversing almost suddenly; no warning. In response she simply cut more lines. The gram was gone within three hours. He demanded more.

It didn't take long for Becks to come back with an eight ball. He eyed it with hunger. After all, the night was young and he'd just fallen in love.

Chapter 9

His urge for cocaine was raging by this point. He was snorting multiple grams every weekend for a month straight. Thanks to the drugs he'd begun drinking a lot more than ever before. It didn't take long for him to show signs of liver damage along his face; exposed by a red rash.

The comedowns had begun to get worse and now he'd do almost anything to avoid experiencing them again. The problem would be solved temporarily with either a few more bumps or a couple of lines. However, the comedowns would soon prove to be inescapable; the inevitable always survived.

The guilt had resurfaced. Sleep was too far away, no matter how he craved for it, it would not come, not until he went through all the motions of despair. His heart would quicken its pace, fear seeping in to his already cracked soul. Oh how the guilt ate him up! He would lie in bed, staring at nothing. At this point nothing felt good. Music could not help him escape, weed didn't work; everything would prove to be fruitless. He knew it was coming, he expected it to, however he'd always underestimate the come down. Always thinking it wouldn't be so bad, that it would go away as quickly as it came. But his comedowns began years ago; this was simply their moment to resurface.

This was his hell; recalling all his pitfalls. Remembering every regret he'd kept in the back of his mind. All those times he'd wished he'd made a right instead of a left. Every wrong step that he'd made, every encounter he wished he'd never crossed. At the center it was always his mother. Yes, it was all his fault. She'd died when he was a failure only to prove to her that he'd remain the same for many more years to come. Oh how he ached to change! Where was the inspiration now? When will he be able to breathe again? Maybe his heart would just pound out of his chest, stopping any further misery from emerging. Death was such a welcoming thought. Only to have it bring along a trusting loyal friend! *Please don't let it be painful!* He'd always thought to himself. Clearly his selfish nature never got lost, only adding to his momentary relapse into darkness. *Will it ever end?*

He got up from his bed with more effort than a handicapped veteran. The blade was always safely stashed in the most convenient of places. The bath wouldn't take long to fill up. The cold metal against his warm skin felt so real. Yet, it was not enough to make it all go away. Not enough to provide him with the escape he'd so desperately needed. Looking up at the mold-speckled ceiling he knew he wouldn't go through with it.

Getting up with the water dripping from his drenched shorts he walked back to his bed only to continue to face the remorse that had always encumbered him. Yes, it would go away, this wont last forever. It began to float out of him. Oh how the sleep overcame him! How he embraced it!

This was his heaven.

Chapter 10

The pain of his last come down was enough for Griffin to decide to never do drugs again. He told Becks to keep it away from him and to not mention a single word about it. She, of course, obliged. She did not question his sudden decision to stop; but she did understand that he had experienced a larger need for the drug than she ever did. She supported him.

"What are you going to do for a job now?" Becks was also concerned about his dwindling finances.

"I'll figure it out today"

"What do you mean 'figure it out' you have to do something. It's only the afternoon I'm sure if you go out right now the recruitment office will still be open"

"That's exactly my plan. I don't know if they'll give me a job though, what use am I to them?"

"I'm sure they need people for at least something. The war is still in full force and the more people they have the better."

"Listen Becks, no offense but you've been on the run the past few years. What do you know about their need for people? They don't need soldiers like me; they've already explained that I'm no good for that. Believe me I've tried to fight, I wasn't good enough"

"Not for the front lines. I understand that you have no military training and right now is too late to start, but they have bases all over the country. They need people for simple jobs. I'm sure of that. Just ask."

He grabbed his jacket and left the apartment. He was pissed off at her. He can do better than some "simple job" he was meant for more than that. She just didn't understand that the world was neither willing nor ready to see his talents. He did not want to waste his time on some bullshit. But his lack of cash weighed heavily on his shoulders. Becks was right. He should put his pride aside and try to get a job; any job, he needs to eat after all.

He made his way to the downtown recruitment office. The place had significantly changed since the last time he had been there; several years ago. He remembered the feel of patriotism and hope that had filled the entire office in the past. There had been lines of young men and women waiting to do their part for their country. Now, the place was empty. Towards the back sat only one officer. He barely resembled an officer. He could not have been any younger than sixty years old. Griffin made his way towards the lone officer. His anxiety suddenly spiked and he simply stood next to the desk at which the officer sat.

"How can I help you?" The officer answered with no enthusiasm. Either the long years of war had washed him out or he just no longer cared.

"I need a job." Griffin replied as he took the seat in front of the officer.

"Listen kid, I don't know why you're here but just turn around and walk back. Whatever job I can give you, trust me, you don't want it."

"The arms factory just closed, I need to live on something. I'll work any job you give me, please." He was ready to beg.

"Too many lives have been ruined. This war took everything from everyone. This isn't a world anymore. We have no freedom, no hope, this isn't life. Why are you so apt on getting a job through the military? Can't you see that it's our fault this has all happened to begin with?"

"I need money for food. There's nowhere else I can go."

The officer stared at Griffin for what felt like no less than five minutes. His own mind could not grasp the concept of working for a life. He had given up a long time ago, but looking at Griffin he understood that even though the rest of the world was in ruins, society still demanded money for food.

"What's your name?"

"Griffin Scoarse"

"What are your qualifications?"

"I worked at the weapons factory in midtown. Before that I'd held several jobs here and there at various food venues."

"Food venues huh? You know how to wash dishes and mop floors?"

"Of course" Griffin accepted his reality at that moment. No matter his skill set, or how highly he thought of himself, in order to survive he'd have to take a simple job.

"I'll have to check with my superiors but I'm sure I can get you a job at the barracks in Brooklyn. You'll mostly be responsible for cleaning up after the soldiers. Washing floors, dishes, laundry, and so on. Come back tomorrow, we'll go over the details then."

"Thank you" Griffin walked out with some hope as he lit his cigarette.

PART TWO

Chapter 1

"Alex Nessler, my name is Kirk Michaels. I'm the lawyer appointed to your case."

"Have you looked at the file?" She said as she drummed her fingers on the cold table in the interrogation room.

"Yes, I have Miss. Nessler."

"Then you already know that I'm guilty. Get a plea bargain or whatever it is that you lawyers do. There is no need for you to work on a defense; besides, all you court appointed lawyers don't really care all that much any way. I just made your job that much easier."

"That is where you're wrong Miss Nessler. I've read over your case multiple times in the last few hours. Something struck me as rather odd. We will plead in any way you wish to do so, however, I believe you're far from being simply guilty."

"What makes you say that?" She eyes the lawyer with curiosity. He was tall, handsome for a burnt out suit.

"Well for one, you do not have a history of violent behavior. You have never been in trouble with the law."

"Go on..."

He let out a small smile before continuing.

"People do not just wake up one day and decide they are going to commit murder, not one like yours. Murderers are often made, sculpted, they are calculating and yet irrational"

"So what makes you think I'm not a murderer? I killed a man. I believe that makes me a murderer."

"Not in the usual sense. You chose a victim who many would agree deserved to die. A known rapist in the neighborhood. To add to that, there was nothing to imply self-defense, the man was shot. One bullet, right in the back of the head. After shooting him you called the cops and turned yourself in. You planned this. You wanted to get caught and go to jail, however, you're not evil, you chose someone whose absence would make society a better place. Some would describe you as a vigilante..." He paused then. Watching her intently for several long seconds before speaking again.

"I'm just wondering why you're so intent on going to prison. I believe there's a psychological reason here, that's the defense."

"So lawyers are psychiatrists now?" She asks with amusement. *The guy's good.*

"I can play this game Miss Nessler. We have time. You exhibit sociopathic tendencies—it's like you're trying to be someone you're not"

"Maybe that's exactly who I am; a cross between a killer and a regular human entirely capable of remorse—an empathetic sociopath"

"But you're not empathetic; rather not sympathetic—you understand the pain of others; that's where your regret comes in, but you can't feel what they feel, can you Miss Nessler?"

"What's your point Mr. Michaels? No matter what you think or the reasons as to why I did what I did, in the end, I still killed a man in cold blood. I'm going to prison."

"I am very capable of defending you Miss Nessler. I can get your sentence reduced maybe even changed. There's a way around this, you do not have to go to prison."

"What if I don't want my sentence reduced? I belong in prison."

Ignoring her, he went on. "You will meet with a qualified psychiatrist, after that we will review your case. Your calm demeanor is of concern. I can see right through your act Miss. Nessler. You've lost hope haven't you? Believe me, you do not want to go to jail." With that he gathers up his papers and exits the room.

Alex Nessler stares at the back of the man who can see right through her. She's dumbfounded. No one has ever been able to characterize her as accurately as he has. Of all the court appointed lawyers in New York and she gets the only one who seems to have a genuine interest in her case. Everything she planned for so long may just backfire.

The psychiatrist came later that evening. It doesn't take long for Alex to finally reveal the truth. At this point, she's got nothing to lose. Yes, she killed a man who deserved to die. The lawyer was right she had lost hope; she had given up a long time ago. This was her way out. She was incapable of suicide in the conventional sense. *Prison: that was her suicide; her personal suicide.* She needed an escape from her life, or lack thereof. This was her only escape; to live out the rest of her life behind bars. Where she'll never have to live up to anyone's expectations. Never have to deal with failure or disappointment. Yet, with her depressed state of mind, Alex Nessler always looked for amusement wherever she could find it. After telling the psychiatrist everything and knowing the defense her lawyer was going to make, she prepared a speech for the jury. If they believe her, no matter how good Michaels is, she will go to prison and finally get some rest.

Chapter 2

The trial took place several weeks after the initial meeting between Nessler and Michaels. The defense was centered on Alex's psychological state. The purpose of which was to reduce her sentence from murder in the first degree to manslaughter. Everything was going in the favor of the defense. The prosecution was not prepared, they have never heard of a case such as this one. However, there was one source they employed which they heavily relied on for the case. The prosecution called Dylan Fintley to the stand as one of their character witnesses.

"No one ever really knew Alex. I'd been sleeping with her for several months and I still don't know her. That's the way she liked to keep things. In a way, she was everybody's best friend, she portrayed herself as some else in front of different people, different situations. Overall, you step back and realize she's still a stranger. You can know her for years and never really know her, who she is, what she likes. We'd go to different bars with different people and her usual drink was never the same. I still can't tell you what her favorite beer is. I'm not saying she was evil, she was never out to hurt anyone, maybe she did this because she never trusted anyone to know her, really know her. But in the end, she's a manipulator, a liar, an actress. That was part of her charm, not too many people ever figured it out though"

Alex wasn't remotely surprised by Dylan's testimony. There was a certain regret she carried around with her in regards to their relationship. He had told her loved her, wanted nothing more than to be with her. To spare his feelings, she had lied. For months she'd tell him what he wanted to hear and he was never suspicious about a single word. He'd look at her as if he couldn't believe that she was with him, that she chose him, and for that, he'd tried to hold on to her as hard as he could. After some time, she couldn't stand it anymore. The sex was repulsive to her; she couldn't bare him touching her. She began to despise him for his feelings, everything he did annoyed her. So, she ended it and finally told him the truth; the relationship was a lie. Clearly, he still hasn't forgiven her.

Soon enough it was time for Alex to take the stand. She and her lawyer had gone over her testimony hundreds of times. She knew what he wanted her to say; the truth. But, Alex Nessler rarely ever did what she was told, whether it was in her best interests or not. She had a plan and she was going to see it through. After being sworn in she begins her act.

She turns her head slowly to the left with no expression on her face as she looks at the jury. She never takes her eyes off of them throughout her speech.

"I remember riding in subway cars, the sweat of the man sitting next to me threatening the burger I had just eaten to violently spurt out of my mouth. I watched the other passengers. They were uglier that day when compared to others, or maybe I just never noticed before. I stared at each and every one of them. I wondered why they were there, why they were in that specific cart, on that train. Why must they all crowd around me? Around my space?"

She paused for a few seconds here, wondering why no one was stopping her. She continued.

"I began to think to myself; why are these people here, these ugly, disgusting, useless people. Not a single one of them has ever made a real contribution to society. Our world was going to shit and they don't even care, either that or they're all just too ignorant to realize it. I am well aware that I did not know a single one of these individuals, yet, I knew they were stupid just like most of the rest of the population. Yes, I believe everyone is an idiot; the people in this room are no exception."

She was ranting now, enjoying the silence of the rest of the room. All eyes on her, all ears on her words.

"Either way, I remember how I felt on that day, in that moment. God, how I hated them. They were breathing the same air as I was, they were breathing *my* air! I stared at the woman across from me. She's crazy sitting across on this train with her gold rimmed glasses covered in two sweaters; one pink the other brown, the latter hanging sloppily off her right shoulder. I can see her zebra print bag on the floor of the subway cart collecting even more filth, unlike her many Duane Reade shopping bags filled with some sort of chocolate bars that she not only feeds to herself but also insists on offering to the strangers around her; they all politely decline. How I wanted to make her suffer, to hear her scream, to beg me for her life as I held it in my hands and slowly let it drip right out of her. I wanted her to feel my pain but on a physical level. I wanted her to die and I wanted to be the one to make that happen."

At this point, Alex Nessler slowly begins to form a smile at the jury with her head cocked to one side, exhibiting insanity in her eyes. She's still surprised that no one had stopped her.

She then notices the smile on Michaels' face. He's got a triumphant look in his eyes as he begins to speak.

"Ladies and gentlemen of the jury, as you can see, my client has quite an avid imagine. None of these events actually took place. This goes to solidify our earlier point on the part of the defense; she has given up in life and would do anything to secure a spot for herself in prison."

Alex stared at him completely baffled. She had lost all composure in her face as the astonished expression she now wore completely gave her away. *How the hell did he do that? How did he know?* She gave up yet again. This time, she'll let someone else win; she can admit defeat, especially to someone who outsmarts her. The guy really was good.

Chapter 3

Keep your head down. Stay invisible.

It was almost breakfast. The COs turned towards the main hall, walking past all the cells. Peering in, leering at them as they slowly got out of bed. Not that there was much to look at from most of the women here. Those in their prime however, got the worst of it.

Sneering at her through the bars as the cells slowly opened, one of the older male COs watched her as she climbed out of bed. With his gut hanging from above his belt, the buttons running down his shirt threatening to fly off as he inhaled and exhaled. She pulled the thin, starchy sheet of a blanket off her, revealing nothing. She slept with her sweats on, rarely ever taking them off.

Now it was her turn to sneer, reveling in his sudden disappointment when instead of seeing her thin naked legs accompanied by small white panties, all he got were those oversized gray sweats. She smiled briefly at his resentment toward her as she walked by him, toward the cafeteria.

"Dyke" he snarled after her as she passed him. She never did understand why the other girls chose to show themselves off in a place like this. Yes, after sometime, needs grow, the demand to satisfy them accelerates. But like this? The thought of him ever touching her...she could feel the rage beginning to boil over. *Keep your head down. Stay invisible.*

She watched quietly, listened every night as others were strapped down. Strapped down for their "own safety" or so they were told. Listened to their muffled cries, muted screams.

Others on the other hand, voiced the other sound of the spectrum. Some excited for the attention, wet with arousal from the touch of any man...or woman.

Here, it wasn't the guards you had to fear. It wasn't the other inmates. No, it was you. You knew what they were capable of, there were no surprises here. It's how you handle it, handle yourself. Getting raped, beaten and in some cases even murdered...that was all on you. *Keep your head down. Stay invisible.*

"Hey there sweetie" one of the resident inmates gestured towards her as she focused on an empty table towards the back. Nodding in acknowledgement, Alex continued to walk forward.

"Where do you think you're going? Why don't you sit here with us?" It was more of a command, not so much a friendly invitation. Alex knew what declining could mean for her. She also knew what sitting with a clique group would do to her.

Keep your head down. Stay invisible.

She looked down at her tray, Styrofoam with plastic utensils. The same you she'd had in elementary school for lunch. Smiling, she sat down at the same table with the group of women. These were white, older, the ones with outside connections.

"Tells us about yourself sweetheart. What's your name?" she had straw, blonde hair. Over-dyed and dried out from years of damage.

"Alex Nessler" she managed to say.

"Nessler huh? Well aren't you pretty." She leaned towards Alex, her hand moving towards her head, caressing her hair as she spoke.

Alex patiently waited for the right moment. Grabbing her plastic spork she made sure to subtly break off the outer crown, creating a jagged edge. Running it back and forth across her left wrist under the table, she let the women stare her down, comment in her direction. She slid the plastic long enough to feel that warm drip run across her skin. Thick enough in consistency, she slowly got up.

Keep your head down. Stay invisible.

"I'm sorry, I cut myself..." she exclaimed as she rose, displaying the blood across her arm, staining her pant leg.

She turned quickly then, walking toward the infirmary. Not looking back, she knew they hadn't bought it, knew she wanted to be left alone. She only hoped they understood this, she wasn't going to frame them, she wasn't a nark.

******

"Why am I getting calls from the psych ward regarding your mental instability Miss. Nessler?" Michaels was more curious than worried it seemed.

"I had to get out of a bad situation, I did what I had to do." He accepted this without any further comment, quickly switching the direction of their conversation.

"The war has begun Miss. Nessler. As your lawyer I've managed to make certain arrangements for an early release."

"Alright, I'm interested."

"As you may have heard, the recruitment has already begun. The military is low on soldiers. They will institute a draft soon. The first place they will look is the prison system. You do not want to be a soldier on the front line. If you agree to serve your country voluntarily, you will gain proper training while they are still able to provide it. And, you'll get out of here."

Prison was not what Alex had anticipated. She'd expected

to wake up at a scheduled time every morning, kill time in her cell, keep to herself as she did the labor outdoors, and go to sleep when told. She had not considered the other inmates. She needed to get out of here. Two years of this shit was enough. War may not be the most luxurious of solutions, but it was a way out.

"I'll do it. I'll sign up for the armed forces. Why on earth the military thinks it's a good idea to give an inmate a gun, I'll never understand, but I won't question it. When do I start?" She was desperate then and didn't care to make any effort to hide it.

"I'll send over the papers by tonight. The recruitment process will take a few weeks. From there we'll get you out of here and into an army base to begin your training. The military, as I've said before, will not be in the position to offer much training once the draft is enforced. The government needs man power, they don't care how equipped those men are. Right now, they can fully train you for warfare. Your case is not one of cruelty. They see a good chance for behavioral reform. If you are willing, they believe you'd make a good soldier."

"A good soldier, Mr. Michaels?"

"Yes, you will be trained to not look at the enemy as human beings but rather as targets. Based on your psychiatric assessment before the trial, you show great promise for the ability to dehumanize others."

"Fascinating, I'm glad my hatred for most of the human population and lack of sympathy is beneficial to the armed forces."

"Glad to hear it, Miss. Nessler." He smiled. "Now that that's settled, let's discuss your personal welfare."

"Like what?"

"Have you been writing Alex?"

"It's the only thing that gets me through the days."

"Good. Keep at it. I'd love to read it some time."

"I plan to burn the pages the second I get out of here Mr. Michaels. I'd prefer not to have anyone read a word of what I've written."

"There's a beauty to your sadness, Alex."

Chapter 4

Her writing wasn't one of false ideals. There lay no conceptual sentences within the pages, no concrete stories. She never wrote of her days or fictional characters to carry on her untold story. In those words lay her truth and solely hers, words never meant for the eyes of others. She wrote what she could not say.

Pages upon pages filled with honest feeling. Words she wished she had been brave enough to speak to those who deserved to hear them. It was her release. She knew it would never be enough, but it was too late to change her past mistakes. If she could go back, tell her mother she was sorry and that she'd never meant to disappoint her, she would. If she was able to turn back the clock and recite to her sister just how often she worried for her, how much she hoped to inspire her, how proud she was of her achievements, she would.

If by some miracle she was capable of looking her boyfriend in the eyes and finally say she loved him, tell him so he can hear the words resonate, let him know how she truly felt, maybe she would never have had to end it all out of fear of never being worthy of his affections. *She would have been anything as long as he'd asked for it.* Reality was not inclined toward miracles. Alex understood this. Though the guilt and regrets she had accumulated over the years never seem to leave her conscience, putting pen to paper made it all just a bit more tolerable.

Michaels was right. There is a beauty to her sadness. Alex would never see this beauty. She was incapable of self praise, never understanding what it was that others saw in her. Often she'd put on a facade, a front, pretend she was someone else. Aside from the rare few who saw right through her, no one really knew who she was. She mimicked every emotion when she felt it was necessary, never truly feeling it. Others might call her an actress, some a manipulator, she herself saw it as an execution of bullshit.

The truth however, was not of deception. She was scared, scared of being herself and being rejected by those around her. So, she gave people what she thought they wanted to see. A smile during happy hour when surrounded by friends; fake down to the last visible tooth. If anyone had ever bothered to really look, they would've seen the sadness in her eyes. It was easier to be someone else than herself. Yes, she was rarely ever herself. Only the eight by ten piece paper marked in gray saw her completely naked, uncovered, and vulnerable.

Only those closest to her, those she truly loved, were able to receive glimpses of who she really was. In the silence resided Alex Nessler's honest form; her true personality. Griffin Scoarse was one of the lucky few. But, it was this lack of execution in her true self, in her failure to verbalize her love for him that had drove them apart. She had ended their relationship not because she did not care, but because she cared too much. He deserved more than what she thought she was able to offer him. He deserved a girl who could say I love you and not lose her voice in the process of doing so. Yes, she would have been anything as long as he'd asked for it. *He never did ask.*

Amongst the pages of disorganized, chaotic emotion, lay the letters she had written to him. She had heard about the bombing in the city about a year ago, and soon discovered that Mrs. Scoarse was one of the victims. She wanted, more than anything, to be there for him. But she knew better than to reach out to him, especially from penitentiary walls. He wouldn't want to be comforted by her; the cold, callous, bitch who took off to only end up behind bars—a murderer.

Instead, she'd written to him. In those letters she was finally able to tell him just how much she cared for him, how strongly she loved him. She explained why she left him, her disappointment when he let her leave, and why she eventually did what she did to end up here.

She never did make up her mind as to whether or not to send those letters to him. She just kept them. Now, as she was emptying out her cell in preparation for her release from prison to the barracks, she once again debated if she should ever give him those letters. She wondered how he was, what he was doing with his life. A part of her worried that he would face the draft, the last thing she would ever want is for him to be put into a dangerous situation. At the same time, if he did end up fighting, there was a small chance that she may be able to see him yet again. She did not humor that ideal fantasy for too long. She packed the letters with the rest of her writing.

She would be free any minute now. Her initial plan to burn her writing suddenly did not seem as appealing as it had just a few weeks ago. Making sure to keep the pages secure and together, she hid them amongst the few articles of clothing and books that she possessed. She was not ready to destroy what she had created, but would never entertain the idea of allowing another to see those words. She would decide what to do later. Right now, she had to focus on getting out and trying to understand how it is that she could ever possibly be capable of fighting a war.

Chapter 5

"Let's begin your psychoanalysis Miss. Nessler" spoke a frumpy old woman in her white lab coat, making sure Alex had given her, her full attention.

"Why? You're going to send me out there anyway, what's the point of checking how insane I am. We've been through this before. Nothing's changed since the last time you decided to 'psychoanalyze' me."

"Miss Nessler this isn't about how insane you happen to be in the present moment. As we've explained prior this is part of your training. Not your physical stamina but your mind. You need to be able to see the opponent as an enemy you must shoot down. Not as a human being. We must erase all weakness from your thinking.

"We'll begin with a routine cross examination Miss Nessler." Alex nodded that she understood.

"Now, do you know why you're here?"

"Yes, I had an option—either rot in a cell or fight."

"Why were you in prison Miss Nessler?"

"I needed a way out, I killed a man."

"How do you feel about war?"

"I don't know" She was getting tired and agitated by the questions now. "It happens, it's human nature. Can't fight it so you just fight…"

****

Dr. Lorens lead Alex into a plain white room. The walls

representing a cell more than a space meant for medical examination. Inside stood one television set with a chair right in front. She inserted a disc and hit play. As she did so she quietly exited the room and locked the windowless door behind.

The video began to play.

After a few seconds of gray static, a woman came upon the screen. It was a frenzied looking woman, with disheveled auburn hair and an orange jumpsuit. She spoke to the camera without any recognition of another soul nearby. Her words carried with them a sense of calm and intelligence, a complete contrast to her physical appearance.

"I watched the blood gather around me. Wash into an endless pool of darkness. Continuously growing, never having the chance to turn brown, lifeless. I watched it wash away my skin, eat away at my muscles and meat, consume my bones. It continued to flow over me, their death, their blood, giving me life.

"I gave them something I may never have. I'm envious of each and every one of them. I gave them a name. I gave them life beyond death.

"They were loved and that love will shine through. I made them memorable. I gave them a voice, be it the voice of a victim but a voice nonetheless. There will be hundreds at their memorial. They will be written about, remembered. Faces upon faces will come to their funerals to mourn. Tears will be cried and sleepless nights will be had, all at their memory. I gave them that. They would never have received it otherwise.

"Without me they would have stayed as nobodies. Possibly have died at old age, having lived through this hell we call life. No one would have remembered them. Few would have cared to see them go.

"I gave them what I cannot have. I took their meaningless lives and made it into something.

"They will forever be seen as innocent victims. Me, I'll be devil. You'll call me crazy, insane, psychopathic. So be it, at least I have accomplished something.

"I miss watching their dying faces, contorted by torture and pain. I'll miss their pathetic pleas; their useless begging. I'll miss holding their life in my hands as I gave them immortality."

She went on to describe her victims in detail. The children, the young girls. How she slaughtered them like cattle. She unflinchingly continued to elaborate on her brutal crimes, with an air of justification.

"You see I wanted to skin them alive, but there had been far too much blood loss with the first few when I had tried. I learned to pace myself. Skin them little by little, let days go by before proceeding to another part of the body. I enjoyed pulling out their little fingernails and teeth, one by one, slowly. Made sure they felt every moment of it."

She carried herself with such certainty you'd think she was entirely sane. The video went on in the same fashion. After about an hour, Dr. Lorens reentered the rom.

"Who was she was Miss. Nessler?"

"I cannot tell you who, but I know what."

"Yes?"

"She was a sociopath."

"Very good, Miss. Nessler."

Chapter 6

"This wasn't supposed to happen. I should never have been here. Can you hear the screams? How can you not? The bombs continue to go off, one right after the other, all followed by those horrid agonizing screams. It's the stuff they never even considered before, never having entered your train of thought. No movie, book, nothing ever came close. This is beyond the nightmares of our childhood, beyond anything we could have ever imagined. And yet, here we are, alive and well, if this isn't hell then I don't know what is."

It was late, well past midnight, and Alex was trying to get some rest before training began at five am. For weeks all she'd wanted to do was rest, just to have a few minutes to herself. Even now, in the bunker she couldn't find an escape from her mental and physical exhaustion.

Bryans never stops talking, his ranting continues all through the night, it's a rarity when snores finally replace his words of unforeseen nightmares. She didn't have that luxury tonight.

"Shut the fuck up Bryans, don't you think that we haven't realized any of this already? Do you really think any of us actually wanted to be here? That any of us wanted to fight, to go to war? Hell, most of us have never even imagined that we'd have to take up the role of soldier, let alone watch all of the people that we once cared about die. They don't even have enough resources or time to train any of us properly, we're getting thrown into a war to die, and each and every one of us is far too ill equipped to actually come out of this thing unscathed in the end, if there even is an end. *None* of us should have ever been here."

Now it's started, Bryans got the others riled up; *there won't be any sleep tonight.* Alex was far too exhausted to deal with the frustration of all the others, all she could now is wait till early dawn and begin the day all over again. She could hope and wish that they would separate the men and women in to different bunkers but such hope was a waste of time and would only lead to disappointment. She chose to save herself from that. The barracks didn't have enough resources to have each one of the bunkers running and made suitable for the soon to be soldiers. What she has to keep focus on is getting as much training in as possible.

The training period will be over by the end of the month, two months is all they get. At least she learned how to shoot; her rifle will remain her last hope. Thankfully, they will all receive plenty of firearms to take into the war, the very war going on in their backyard, in everyone's backyard.

The cold was beginning to have an effect as well. There was no comfort. The boilers stopped producing enough heat to sustain the entire barracks, only the top officials were able to take a hot shower. Not that it would matter anyway; they only got five minutes a day to bathe. There really wasn't much to look forward to anymore besides getting out of the barracks— *and then what? Enter the war where they're all guaranteed to die anyway?* There is a silver lining; at least she's got a purpose. She'll enter that war ready to die but she will fight. She'll give everything she has, and hopefully, take down some of the enemy as well.

Her job will be to protect the oil reserves in Alaska; apparently the Russians are putting up a good fight, enough to make the government nervous. To add to that, Canada had resolved to abstain from a position of neutrality. Now, the Alaskan reserves are under major threats coming from all sides. The rest of the world will not be her problem. However, logic often times keep her head spinning. Even if humanity doesn't kill itself off in the war and they do win this thing after all has been said and done, will they be able to make life sustainable? Even with the resources they may gain from the enemy, it won't be enough. No one on the planet has enough, that's why they're all at war to begin with. Humanity killed off the planet and now that it's dead the last thing left for humanity to kill is itself.

Chapter 7

"They say that all of Western Europe is in chaos. No one knows who their allies are anymore. It's practically a free for all. Every country is getting bombed, the people, the food, the land, it's all destroyed. They're warning us that pretty soon France and Germany are going to attack us here and join the Koreans and Japanese. Forget the middle east, its mass extinction out there."

Alex listened as she ate the colorless shit they called food. "How are they even organizing this war?"

"That's the point, they're not. It's every man for himself."

"How can they continue on with the destruction? It's complete chaos. You'd think the intelligence of human beings would have done things differently. That somehow we would have come together to not only sustain ourselves but to help the planet survive, not do the complete opposite."

"That would contradict humanity. We have always been violent; people killing people just to get ahead. Why would this be any different? It's the end of the world after all, if you want to survive then you have to be an animal, all instinct, forget that bullshit of peace on earth, that has never happened and it never will."

"Why bother sending us to Alaska anyway then? What's the point?"

"Let them believe what they're doing is right. In my opinion, they should have given us the guns and instructed us on how best to pull the trigger when it's aimed at our own heads."

This was common talk amongst the soldiers. Morale was low and they have yet to enter the actual war. If there was any hope, any reason to fight, the war itself had stripped that from the soldiers a long time ago. It seemed like a pointless battle, a war that cannot be won, not by anyone. The nuclear waste it's given off has already made parts of the world practically unlivable. Evacuations have been underway since the very beginning, but once point A gets evacuated to point B, they need to evacuate point B to point C, it's endless and nonsensical. But, they will fight, they will pretend. For most of the soldiers, the delusion of a comfortable end is all that kept them going.

It wouldn't be long now, Alex thought to herself. Maybe this was it, the best it was going to get before hurdling completely downhill. She tried not to think about it. Somehow though, it all seemed to have worked out for her in a sick, twisted way. She wanted to go to prison to not have to face her own mundane life, a life that was glorious compared to all the lives now. Prison had not been it, now she's about to go into the war. *Yes*, she thought, *the war would be it.*

She had finally found what she was so desperately searching for. A safe haven away from the responsibilities of a daughter, a sister, a college graduate. She'd be the first to admit that she had been a coward, too scared to face every morning, as it would always inevitably come. Now, they're telling her when to go to sleep, when to wake up, when to eat, when to shower—there was no thinking on her part. The war had already begun keeping her busy and given her some form of direction. In a way, she now had a purpose before it will all end. She had finally found her own personal suicide.

That's why they saw her as the perfect soldier. She can kill the enemy easily thanks to her hatred for most of mankind.

There would be no hesitation, no psychotic break. She learned a long time ago how to separate humanity from a corpse. She wouldn't look at them as individuals, people with families, with their own set of beliefs. No, to her they were all the same, a moving target. But it's not her ability in never having to hesitate before taking a shot that they needed, it was her own personal desire to die. She didn't want to live her life, but she did have a strong urge to survive. It's that survival and lack of fear for her own life that would make her irreplaceable in the line of fire. *Psychologically, she was the perfect soldier.*

Chapter 8

"It's fucking freezing out here. You'd think we'd have gotten used to the cold by now." Bryans complained as they sat around a fire.

There were about seven of them left in the battalion. They had lost all major communications with those back at the home field. However, they knew their job. Keep the Russians out and the Canadians at bay.

"We won't last for much longer, especially not if the Russians get here. They know the cold; they're well acquainted with the snow." One of the others, Lynns, exclaimed.

"Be grateful that it's not their home turf, if we were in Siberia, as history has already shown us twice, we wouldn't have stood a chance." Alex chimed in. A little bit of hope to her empty words. "That or they've always got that vodka on hand to help keep 'em warm." Some laughter brought light to the current situation.

"They should've left us with a few bottles before sending us out here. What are we fighting anyway? I haven't seen any Russians or Canadians for days now. I'm not saying that I'm not grateful for that, no conflict for now, gives us a surviving chance, but it's like a damn camping trip. All we do is hunt and build fires." Bryans seemed anxious. Then again, he always did.

"Glad for the hunt, tonight we've got mountain goat, the other day we got us some venison, I'd say we're eating large over in this part of town."

"Yeah, I agree with Lynns, it could've been worse. The cold's not so bad. Best thing, we've got fire for heat, plenty of food, and enough quiet time to rest. I'd say this is better than training." One of the others added.

Alex wasn't one to complain. She enjoyed the company of the others. But they've been keeping "guard" for several days now with no action. Why would they have been sent here if there was nothing to do, something's not right here. The quiet only makes her more uneasy. She'd have loved to enjoy it, seems likes the only time to actually get some rest. The scenery is rather beautiful, worlds away from the dumps of the cities. Parts of the place seemed to have never been disturbed by humanity at all. Though she knew there are cabins around, cabins that once housed whole families, before the evacuation, before the draft.

She checked and rechecked her rifle every night. It became a ritual, making sure everything was in its rightful place, doubling checking her ammo. They had wasted more bullets on the animals they would feast on than on enemy soldiers. It was good target practice though. They continued to train, to improve their accuracy and reflexes throughout the days. Making good use of the time they had. Well, at least most of them were. All Bryans ever seemed to do was complain. She fantasized of torturing him, choking him, giving him something real to complain it. She'd never felt more annoyed by another human being. She found comfort in her imagination, when everyone else was fast asleep, she'd let it go wild. At times, she'd find herself smiling at the thought of putting a bullet through his fucking head or stabbing him through his right eye; anything, to just shut him up forever.

She hid her disdain quite well, not just from Bryans but from the rest of the soldiers as well. She came off as amiable, reasonable, and always deep in thought. Someone not to be bothered, only entering conversation with valued input, never wasting breathe on pointless words. Unlike Bryans who didn't seem able to ever keep his mouth shut. *They all had to deal with the cold, that selfish annoying pig.* For now though, she had other things on her mind. She didn't have the energy to waste on Bryans and his personal weather forecast.

The lack of warmth wasn't much of an issue for her, the fire kept her warm enough to get through the nights. There haven't been any storms either, to that she was grateful. Maybe it really is all in her head. The quiet is normal, not something to fear. Though, she still couldn't shake off that feeling that something's wrong. It shouldn't be this quiet, this peaceful... *The quiet before the storm.*

Chapter 9

Morning was just setting in as the early dawn cold woke her from a restless sleep. She couldn't stop thinking of her last conversation with Michaels. A wave of guilt washed over her as she continued to dwell on their last encounter.

He had come to see her before she was to be shipped off for duty, a final goodbye before her departure. Her reaction was not one that had resulted in pride.

Michaels came in to check on her welfare, make sure everything was all right before she had headed off to combat. His comments of reassurance and questions focused on her personal wellbeing resulted in a defensive attack from Alex's side.

She spoke of her choices, her lack of regret in making them. For the first time she completely let her guard down around him. She tried explaining what he already knew but couldn't accept. She wasn't the type to live a "normal" life; that it had all gotten too much for her. That her fear of failure is the sole reason why she couldn't bare the responsibilities of a regular job, learn to be independent as society viewed it by staying forever dependent on a paycheck. Having to constantly make those who cared for her proud while appeasing total strangers.

"Is that why you went to prison? You needed a way out?" He condescendingly asked.

"I went to prison because I fucking killed someone. Stop treating me like some special case. I can assure you that I'm not that interesting. Just let me go off to war and finish up my time."

"You do realize you might be walking to your death. Don't you feel any fear, any hesitation toward the impending situation?"

"Have I been talking to a fucking wall this entire time? No shit I realize that. Of course I'm scared, who wouldn't be? But this is my decision, this is what I want."

Maybe it hadn't been too bad of a conversation; it wasn't exactly an argument. Her regret stemmed from an emotional consequence; she took from Michael's the simple good bye he had come looking for.

****

The rest of the camp was slowly waking up to the Alaskan brisk wind. She had already prepared their breakfast, the same goat from last night, reheated.

Lynns grabbed his bowl and began spooning in his breakfast. "When do you think this will end? Are we ever going to go home, go back to normal?"

"I don't think it will ever be normal, this is the new normal."

"You're right, but why bother at this point?"

"You know why, we need the resources. The whole world needs resources; mankind no longer has a sustainable environmental yield. We're all fighting to survive, fighting our enemies so our government can provide for us."

"Our government, Alex? Where the hell is that government? This war is their fault to begin with. They should have known we were consuming at an exponential rate, using up every resource the planet had offered. We left nothing, nothing for future generations to live on. Every government is guilty of ignorance, of inaction when we needed it most.

At this point, everyone is an enemy. There are no front lines, no bridges, no concrete national army—for *any* nation. You don't know who you're fighting out there. It's just fighting and killing—war—a justified murder...a massacre that will never be admitted as such. We're bringing the entire human race closer to extinction. We've depleted our natural resources, destroyed this planet, no we're destroying ourselves. This is survival of the fittest to the extreme, only now we're an endangered species living on an unsustainable planet. Those who do survive won't be left with much. This war is meaningless; if we don't kill ourselves through warfare then our ignorance has already done so."

Chapter 10

There's only one thing we know to be certain, and that's death. There's a relief, a beauty to that. You take that away and we're lost.

They'd held a seminar for the soldiers before leaving home base; a special guest speaker had been invited. A final chance to remind them all that death is necessary, anything beyond that shows weakness and failure. Kill the enemy, and you've done your job. No need to overcomplicate warfare.

While they sat around the fire trying to keep warm, she continuously ran those words through her head. It was the last link she had to understanding why she was even out there. It had been seven years now.

We fight this war, just as humanity has always done—war. We're a violent yet strategic species. War is death, without that, we can't fight. How can you fight an enemy that can't be killed? If you can't be killed? What's the fun in that? Then again, mankind has always been innovative, especially in the art of war; a creative solution would be put in place—a means to an end. One that already exists right before we choose to take a life, we call it torture— a gruesome and grotesque method, so very unnecessary and ineffective. It takes away whatever humanity we had left, both from the victim and the executioner. We're all sadists in the end.

The cold continued to grow along with the silence. In the last few years they rarely had to fight, only lifting their guns to ensure their hunger was put off for at least another day. Their war was one of a waiting game.

The five of them sat around the fire, same as they had every day prior. Lynns, Bryans and Alex sat on one side as Krip and Franklin sat on the other.

The howls of wind were the only sounds they heard as Franklin slumped over onto the ground. The pure white snow was slowly turning red around his body. There had been no sound, no warning of attack.

They were not prepared. After seven years, the thought of combat had become a distant one.

"Run!" Bryans yelled to the others as Krip's left shoulder was grazed by yet another bullet.

Another five seconds and silent bullets were flying all around them, from every direction possible. They were finally under attack.

The four of them ran through the snow in to the nearby woods for cover. The wind penetrated through their gear and exposed their faces to the severe cold. Adrenaline and fear rushed through them as they made their way to safer surroundings.

The soft snow sunk them deeper, making the half-mile run seem longer than it really was. With every footstep, they lost more and more strength; their breath became heavier as they pushed through.

"Nessler, did you grab the guns?" She had been closest to the weaponry, the rifles only feet from her.

"Only two handguns, I didn't have a chance for more." Her failure to produce in that moment left her feeling useless, regret quickly overcame her fear.

"What the hell!" Bryans screamed as a bullet penetrated through his right thigh. His pace quickly slowed as he struggled to catch up with the others. In a split second, Krip was lying face down in the snow. He was gone.

"Bryans you're lagging behind! Hurry the fuck up!" Lynns yelled from over twenty feet in front.

Alex stopped running in that moment. She had to turn back, needed to help Bryans speed up his pace before they were all dead. Running towards him, he gratefully allowed her to help him through as he put one arm over her shoulder and the two ran together towards the dense woods.

Lynns was already on the ground by the time they reached safer land. The two collapsed and began to inspect his wound. Alex carefully dug the bullet out of his leg with the one knife she had.

The bullet wasn't something they had come in contact with in the past. They'd never seen anything like it. A blinking red light made it's way to the top point of the bullet.

"They have a tracker! Those fuckers have trackers on their bullets!" Lynns screamed out with fear and frustration. "We need to keep moving, they'll get to us here. Their technology is far superior to our fucking handguns, there's no way we can fight them all. We have to get the hell out of here…NOW!"

"Who the hell do you think that is?" Bryans asked as he struggled to get up.

"The whole fucking world is at war! There are no alliances, only enemies, it could be anyone. Hell it could be our own men!" Lynns responded

"For all we know it could be civilians."

"How the hell did civilians get their hands on this kind of technology? Don't be an idiot, Bryans."

With nightfall getting closer, Alex knew they had to keep moving, if only for hope of life. It chilled her as she realized who their attackers were. No matter what they did or how far they ran, their chances of survival were slim to none. But they had to try.

"These aren't our men..." she told Lynns and Bryans, "they don't belong here. I've heard of this enemy before..."

****

They'd left her there. She was alone now; the thought caused her to break out in chills. She knew what lay ahead. She'd heard the screams, felt her own desperation in her cries. They tied her up, left her on the dirt, rodent infested ground. The stink of urine and feces swallowed her as she began to gag. That sweet sting of blood, dried and fresh, suffocating the walls. With a bag over her head, they left her there, the darkness only bringing light to her fear. She heard the door shut as footsteps approached her.

They'll keep her alive long enough to ruin her completely, to scar her in every way possible. Long enough for her to never think of escape, but rather, to beg for death—her only way out, her only true escape...as it had always been.

PART THREE

Chapter 1

The barracks are a filthy place of employment. The soldiers encased within these walls often find themselves ill with their own grime, though they rarely notice it. However unaware they are, the outsider's eye is not blind to the inhabitants' muck. Griffin may be an outsider, but he is no stranger to the gruesome dwellings in which these men and women are confined.

What does surprise him however, is the lack of self within those brick and tile imprisonments. They are entirely unaware of what it is—a prison. Some act as if it's a safe haven. *And, why not?* There's food, a hot shower, creaking cots overrun with bed bugs which they call beds. For most of the soldiers, their standards are low and expectations often lowered. For Griffin, it's the makings of human ruin.

His first week at the barracks, he was assigned to maintenance—typical janitorial work. He wouldn't have minded as much had he not been the one to scrub the grime off the lavatory rooms. Shit stains were one thing, but there seemed to be no limit to the blood and vomit that speckled the already soot covered tiles. The entire place reeked of death.

The caged dorms in which the men spent their nights were no better. Spit was tossed around and left behind. Snot entering it's way onto the walls and settling deep between the sheets.

Remarkably, the dining area wasn't nearly as decomposed as the remainder of the barracks. He was told to prepare himself for the kitchen after several weeks had been passed;

they needed a new cook. Experience, of course, was not a requirement.

In the meantime, he'd follow his orders. Leave everything as clean as possible, though no matter the amount of bleach that was used and the time his raw knuckles spent scrubbing the place, the stench would never disappear.

"The Alaskan band is on it's way back, we need to prepare their quarters along with making arrangements for the infirmary to be sanitized" His commander informed him. Commander Brint was a short man, insecure with his appearance and made up for it by acting tougher than he really was in this new position of power.

The infirmary was a miserable sector of the barracks. Only cleaned prior to new arrivals. Afterwards, the blood, human decay, and pus is left to dry alongside the cots until the next set of wounded survivors are welcomed.

He reluctantly headed towards the infirmary to take care of the day's tasks. He began by stripping all the cots of their soiled sheets, throwing them into a designated pile meant for the other staff to take care of the laundry. Prepped with bleach and strong alcohol based cleaners he began wiping down the rusted metal of the bedsprings and the metal frames. He'd scrubbed so hard that his fresh blood began mixing with the brown, dried leftovers of the cots' previous inhabitants.

After several hours had passed, the infirmary appeared to be in suitable enough condition for the next wave of soldiers. It wasn't long before they'd arrived.

Only two soldiers entered the infirmary, two men. One appeared to have flesh wounds consisting of stab marks and burns, whereas the other sustained more severe injuries, particularly to his right leg.

One of the resident nurses, the barracks only had three in

its employ, began the busy work taking down their information as they waited for Sergeant Benson to arrive.

"Please state your name and rank" she instructed as she flipped open a notepad.

"Christopher Lynns, Private" the first told her.

"Jason Bryans, Corporal" identified the second.

"Any other soldiers from your company alive?" asked the nurse.

"No, just us" Lynns responded.

"How were you rescued?"

"We made contact with base camp, located in Anchorage, Alaska." Lynns spoke again.

"Are any opposing forces aware of the barracks location here in New York?"

"Not that we are aware of." Lynns said. He appeared to be only one able to speak of the two.

"How many dead from your company that you are aware of?"

"Three"

"How many tortured before death?"

"One"

"Please identify the soldier's name."

"Alex Nessler, Private."

"That would explain the package we'd received earlier today, I believe it was meant for the both of you." Said Sergeant Benson as he entered the room.

"What package?"

"See for yourself private" he pulled in a gurney with what appeared to be a cardboard box, the sides seeping with blood.

Chapter 2

Griffin glanced inside the box as Lynns slowly lifted up the lid. There she was, or what was left of her. Alex Nessler lay there, inside her cardboard casket, mangled and mutilated. She had been delivered to them in pieces.

"Once you're all patched up here, the two of you, we will conduct a formal interview on the events that had occurred over in Alaska. This isn't the first package of this kind we've received." The Sergeant motioned to Lynns and Bryans.

Griffin slowly backed out of the room, careful to hide his emotion from the others. The sickness was building up inside of him. He made for the lavatory. Soon his human waste would mix in with that of the soldiers.

"Scoarse, where are you? We need you in the infirmary" Yelled his commander.

He slowly lifted himself off his knees and let go of the once porcelain bowl. "Coming" he yelled back.

He quickly washed his face and rinsed his mouth before hurrying out.

"We need you in the infirmary, we're low on witnesses. Need someone to take notes."

He made his way back and was handed a notepad, similar to the one the nurse had been using earlier.

"Glad that we're all here, let's begin. Who was the enemy that attacked you, what force were they fighting for?" Asked the Sergeant.

"That was unclear, Sergeant" replied Lynns.

"Who were the soldiers, private?"

"I'm not—" began Lynns before Bryans cut him off.

"The kind of soldiers who have no loyalties, no ties, no government. To them, its survival of the fittest and they fight as such. They fight with no morality, no honor. These men are best described as thieves, rapists, and murderers—they're all convicts. The terrorists of our fathers' time. We never stood a chance."

"What happened out there Corporal? What happened to Private Nessler?"

"They had us, we managed to escape…"

"Not Nessler, I need details."

"You have to understand Sergeant."

"Understand what?"

"Escape…that's all we were able to focus on. It all happened so fast. They had us, she, Alex…she fought back. Lynns and I, we managed to get out…" he hesitated before continuing. "We never took a second to take note of our surroundings. We just ran and kept running. Only thinking of getting out, moving as fast as possible—escaping the tortures happening behind us…I thought she was with us, I wanted to believe she was with us…" he broke down.

They ran and never once considered to turn around. To just glance back and realize she wasn't among them, to pay attention to the defiant screams of a woman. To just listen and hear that those screams escaped her, escaped their savior's throat…Escape and survival was all they could think of, fore that, unfortunately, is apart of the human condition. The natural response, fight or flight. They had chosen flight. Their regret would soon come to haunt them for the remainder of their lives. Guilt and imagination can be worse than any form of physical torture. Torture of the mind is a murderer in and of itself.

Chapter 3

"Hey! Hey You!" He heard a shout, unaware that it was directed at him until a giant ball of slush hit his right arm.

It had been another cold night in New York's winter, snow was falling heavily and traffic was at a stand still. As always on nights like these, the buses crowded the streets, filled with those tired after a long day's work, commuting back to their central heated homes.

The tires were covered in chains, making a snow day in New York more hectic than beautiful.

He looked up and he saw her standing several feet in front him, consumed by her grey snowboarding jacket and fuzzy plaid hat.

"Sorry about that!" she screamed after him, "wasn't meant for you."

"It's alright," he said as he slowly turned to walk away.

"My name's Alex" she was smiling at him, challenging him to come towards her.

He obeyed, "Griffin."

Her cheeks were flushed pink from the cold and her small hands turning red as the snow melted off of them. He would learn later that she wasn't the type to wear gloves, found them to be an inconvenience.

She wasn't alone, she explained to him. Her friends were at a nearby bar; she needed to step out for air.

He offered his company while she walked aimlessly around the blocks of the city. He wanted nothing more than to get home, but something about her left him obligated.

"So, what brings you out here this time of night?" She asked with genuine curiosity.

"Just got out of class" he was surprised himself that he'd even gotten out of his bedroom, especially in this weather. However, he'd had a midterm and forced himself to show up for it.

"Why are you so trusting of a stranger?" He'd asked her.

"We're in the same class" she started laughing then. "You're not a complete stranger, why don't you join us at the bar?" she asked.

He tried to pinpoint her from class, but with his lack of attendance and constant self-involvement it's no mystery that he couldn't place her. To him, she was a complete stranger.

"I can't I really do need to get home." The last thing he needed was to be surrounded by a group of strangers pretending to have fun, only making the atmosphere more awkward around him.

"I understand, well it was nice meeting you Griffin, maybe I'll see you sometime in class?"

"Sure, it was nice meeting you too." As he walked away he made a point to show up more.

Alex Nessler was not someone who'd opened up right away, that was part of her appeal; it only made him want to know her more.

Chapter 4

The bullets suddenly stopped flying as silence filled the Alaskan night air. Alex looked on as the enemy slowly approached them. There must've been at least a dozen men. She glanced at Bryans' leg, the blood continued to stain the snow as it leaked out of him.

"Byrans, you need to start moving, get a head start." She whispered.

"No... I can't leave you behind." He hesitated as he spoke.

"Look, I'll try to hold them off. Lynns and I can run faster than you, we're not handicapped. You need to get a head start if we're all going to get out of here. Lynns, I need you to cover me, I have a plan. But I *need* you to watch my back." She explained as she slowly got up.

"GO!" she yelled towards Bryans as she ran in the opposite direction, towards the enemy line.

A few of the men had raised their guns to take aim, ready to shoot her down as she headed towards them. The snow leaving her more exhausted with every step. She collapsed onto her knees only a few feet away from them.

Two of them made their way over to her, guns raised and pointed at her head. She glanced back at Lynns, reassuring herself that he was still there.

Lynns got his gun ready in case they pulled their triggers. He watched them get closer and closer to her, realizing that if he didn't leave now, he may not make out alive. She'd just given him the distraction he needed to escape.

"Get up bitch," yelled one of the soldiers with absolutely

no accent. American, she realized. She had been right, these men aren't military, they're criminals.

She spit in his face as he began pulling her up by her left arm. In response he broke out in hyena-like laughter. "This cunt thinks she's the shit."

She glanced back again, Lynns wasn't anywhere in sight.

"Are there any others with you?" he asked.

"No, just me."

"Don't lie to me bitch, there were at least two more in your company. Where are they hiding?"

She remained silent. Hoping Lynns would start shooting, at any time now. Her gun was loaded and ready, they hadn't checked her for weapons yet. One of the knives was safely stowed away in her boot. She can feel the sharp blade sliding against her calve. Now, she had to wait. The second Lynns began shooting, she can move to the offensive. *What the hell is he waiting for?*

"Listen whore, we're not playing games. Where the fuck are the rest of them?"

He wasn't patient with her silence.

Bryans was out of breath by the time Lynns caught up with him. "Where's Nessler?"

Lynns ignored the question, "Just keep moving."

Suddenly the silence was broken as the deafening sound of three shots shook up the calm air.

****

Lynns woke up with a jerk, with Bryans asleep on the cot to his right. He would continue to have nightmares on that night, no matter how much time went by, the guilt never lessened. *At least I'm still alive* he thought to himself, willing to say anything to convince himself that he'd done the right thing, that he really had no choice.

He could hear someone right outside the door. He slowly got up and went towards the main hall. Right outside was the janitor he'd seen earlier. A sad looking man, with one leg a little shorter than the other. He appeared to have been crying.

"You all right?" he approached him.

Startled, Griffin looked up and nodded.

"I'm Chris."

"I know. I was there when they were questioning you. My name's Griffin."

"That's right. So, what's there to do around here? Any beers around? I'd kill to play a game of Texas Hold 'em."

"No" Griffin was curt with him, barely able to make eye contact. *How could this dick not have any feeling? He'd just been presented with her severed head and doesn't even seem to care.* "How well did you know Alex?'

"Nessler? Fought alongside her for years over in Alaska."

"How was she, at the end?"

"Why you asking? Did you know her?"

"No, just curious. Not everyday you get a head delivered in a box…"

"You've got a point. She was strong at the end, one of the best. They used to call her the perfect soldier."

"Why's that?"

"She was willing to run out into the line of fire, didn't care if she died."

"How'd you make it out of alive? I mean she died, how'd you survive?"

"Like I said, she was the perfect soldier. She took a risk and paid for it with her life. I focused on survival…I got out. That's all."

"You ever think about her? Ever wonder if there was something more you could've done?"

"No. There was nothing else I could have done. I'd have gotten killed along side her. Look, she was a great person, was always willing to make sacrifices for the betterment of the group. The way everything played out at the end, there was no other route to take. If I were able to go back, nothing would change. The outcome would still be the same, she'd still be dead."

"It's a good thing you're alive then." Griffin said with a hint of sarcasm.

"Thanks..." Lynns shrugged as he walked back to the dormitory.

Chapter 5

It was two in the morning by the time he got back to his small apartment in the city. He found Becks in his bedroom, already fast asleep. He needed someone to talk to, anyone. He sat at the foot of the bed staring down at her as her body slowly lifted up and down with breath. She made a small whimper as he tried to wake her, and then thought better of it.

He'll discuss the day's events with her in the morning, before it was time to make his way back to the barracks.

They had given him the option of residence in the dormitories, separate from the soldiers of course. But, he needed a place to escape to, longed for his own bed. Besides, that place always stank of death and piss.

He thought back to the time he and Alex had been together. It had been ages ago, well before the war had even been a topic of conversation. A time when things seemed simple, easy and not so anxious. He recalled her beauty, she never considered herself to be good looking, her low maintenance stance made her even more attractive.

They had been drinking a few beers one night, in his mother's home, out on the fire escape in back. It had been a warm mid-July night. It was just to the two of them and they were only a couple months into their relationship. By that time he had opened up to her completely, she knew everything there was to know of Griffin Scoarse, and still she stayed with him.

She on the other hand, was more remote. Hesitant when it come to her own life. That is, until that night. She still hadn't told him much but she finally opened up about her family—about her father.

Some stories of an absentee father centered around abandonment, for Alex that had not been the case. Her story was focused on abuse and neglect.

He'd been a heroin addict, and as far as Griffin knew still was. The guy had a way of simply not dying. Alex recounted one story involving him that struck Griffin hard, amongst the memories of abuse there was one in particular that he simply couldn't forgive.

When she had ben five years old and ill with the flu, he had promised her mother that he'd take Alex to see the doctor. It had been February and below freezing on that day in particular. She recalled holding his hand as they walked down the street toward the train station. She didn't think anything of it until they made a right about three blocks short of the subway entrance.

After walking for another ten minutes he stopped and instructed her to stand on the street and wait for him, *he'd be right back, he'd promised.* He turned the corner and she just stood there in the cold. No hat, no gloves, only a small jacket entirely unsuitable for the winter. He rarely cared what she was dressed in before leaving the house.

She stood on that street for hours, waiting for him to finally return. A little five year old girl, alone on a street corner in Brooklyn standing through the bitter cold. He did eventually make his way back, but by that time daylight had already been gone for several hours.

She'd been shivering from the cold, scared to go find heat, afraid that he wouldn't find her—or worse get upset with her and "teach her a lesson" when they did make it home.

Her mother had been hysterical by the time they'd made it

back. He had instructed Alex to lie for him, to explain that there had been a long line at the pediatrician's office. She did as he asked, always obedient. Her mother knew better. She could see he was high.

The sight of her daughter shivering all over with red cheeks and purple lips was enough for her to go off the deep end.

Before she can reprimand him however, he'd begun beating her right in front of Alex. This was a regular occurrence for the family.

Her mother always working and her father abusing the both of them in between highs, was a daily routine. Alex spoke of how her mother would work long nights, coming home to get at least a couple of hours of sleep before leaving for her second job in the morning. How she'd desperately try to hide the money she'd made so she can put food on the table before he had a chance to beat it out of her.

That had been their life until finally her mother gained the courage to move out and they both left him. He still hadn't left their lives entirely, not until Alex had been in High School, by which point she didn't even view him as a human being.

When Griffin asked if he'd ever sobered up, Alex looked straight ahead, not meeting his gaze as she spoke; "That's the only life he knew. Sobriety was never an option, sobriety meant responsibility, something he was never able to handle. Drugs were his excuse, they still are. And, they will continue to be his excuse until the day he finally dies."

She was very matter of fact when she spoke of her father, never revealing any form of emotion. He recalled having tears well up in his eyes, as his throat got dry and his chest heavy. He was crying for her, but she didn't appear to have any emotion at all. When it came to her father, she felt exactly as she spoke: numb.

Chapter 6

This isn't the first package of this kind we've received.

Griffin kept picturing the moment the box had been delivered, constantly recurring with the blood always seeping through, more poignant each time he thought of it.

On the commute over to the barracks, he tried to get some sleep. Memories of Alex kept flooding into his head making it impossible for him to just let go and let the exhaustion take over.

No matter how hard he tried, sleep was nowhere in sight. He'd have to carry on with his daily routine consumed by fatigue, get through the day on autopilot.

As on most mornings, he made his way into the kitchen. This morning's breakfast consisted of pre-cooked, prepackaged oatmeal. He referred to it as slimy grains of cardboard as he stirred it into the pot of boiling water. The soldiers never seemed to mind though as they scarfed down their portions of the grey glop.

He couldn't wait to get out for the day, see Becks and pass out. But in the meantime he was on kitchen duty. After a half hour the colorless paste begun bubbling over the pot. Griffin removed the giant pot from the heat and began ladling it into the white ceramic bowls provided. Towards the eighth bowl he began dazing off, lost in his thoughts of Alex and what the sergeant had meant by this not being the only package received.

He knew he couldn't enter certain areas of the barracks. All the soldiers had been implanted with a chip in their left wrists.

Only with these chips can they gain access to the dormitory they were assigned to and other parts of the barracks. Of course, several of these men were given access to the entire sanction, one being the sergeant.

Everyday, in between shifts he'd have to wait to be let in to the rooms his duties were scheduled to take place, including the lavatories.

He'd heard stories of how the dead had to be burned, the chip somehow destroyed if it was possible to do so.

He began wondering what had happened to those left wrists of the dead soldiers that had been delivered. Those men, who'd killed them, killed Alex, knew of the barracks, but were they aware of the access chips these soldiers had implanted?

He'd lost track of time before realizing the pot had been emptied out. After all the soldiers had been fed, he went into the cafeteria and began gathering up all the trays getting them ready for the washer. As he made the rounds, scooping up sticky tray after tray he noticed that Lynns and Bryans were still in the cafeteria.

As he approached them, their voices grew quiet, careful to not be overheard.

Acting ignorant Griffin went towards them. The two quickly stopped their conversation as Griffin stacked up the trays surrounding them.

"Just out of curiosity" Griffin began, "Do you really have to burn the other soldiers after they've been killed?"

Lynns was a bit sidetracked, as if he'd never heard of such thing. He had a look of confusion sprawled across his face before a sudden realization took over.

Bryans was the first to speak. "Yes, but only if we have the opportunity. We do not risk our lives to do so."

"Is it because of the chip?"

"Yes, but no one besides the American soldiers know about it, as far as I know" as he said those words his face slightly contorted, registering for maybe the first time what they may have missed.

"I know about it, and I'm not a soldier" Griffin pointed out, ignoring the panic in their eyes.

"Yes, well that's because you work here. No getting around it…I'm sorry we have to go" Lynns starting getting up, Bryans following suit.

Since the war had begun, safety and the notion of calm was not an option. However, for the first time since those initial bombs had gone off in the city, Griffin suddenly felt panicked.

If those men are American as Lynns and Bryans had hinted towards, then there's a good chance they are aware of the access chips. They may have their very own, though deactivated if they have been labeled as deserters.

Either way, no one made any mention of where those wrists are, *where those chips are.*

Griffin quickly regained his thoughts, *no the sergeant would have warned them, they wouldn't be here right now if there was any threat, any danger. There's no way no one else couldn't have come to this realization.*

Summing it up to paranoia Griffin continued cleaning off the cafeteria in time for lunch.

But there have been others…

Chapter 7

The verification chip was first developed several years prior to the war. Scientists stationed in a lab in upstate New York were instructed to design and engineer a microchip to be implanted into human skin. The purpose of which was to deal with the national security crisis at hand. They had never imagined that every American soldier would have one within the course of two years.

Bryans stared up at the ceiling of the room he shared with Lynns. Fidgeting slightly in the metallic cot, the springs screeched with his every move.

Every soldier and military official was given an extensive briefing on what the chip was, how it was to be used, and the precautions to take.

He rubbed his left wrist as he remembered the days he'd endured in training. At the time he would never have imagined what the world would inevitably become.

Once a chip is imbedded into the skin of the host, activation occurs in a central data depository center—the location of which is known by a very few military personnel and political officials. Prior to the installation the soldier's personal data and demographics are recorded into the system.

He'd given up everything that had once been important to him. Numbers, code, all those zeroes and ones—now gone, at least for him.

Precautions are to be taken to remove and destroy the chip or burn the corpses. Those missing and dead are to be reported and acknowledged as soon as possible. In the event of such a report, the main system can terminate the code within the chip from its central location.

Reaching into his pocket he felt for that similar sense of comfort. Something that made him feel like someone more than just a man on the frontline waiting to die.

If a chip is not manually destroyed, there is a brief period of time before the identity is documented and the termination of the verification is chip is completed. Systems are in a state of vulnerability during this period. For the termination process to occur from within the central location all new chips in production must be halted and security experiences various glitches within the access restrictions given per host.

Those days in the training fields, all the mines to be tested, the psychological "prep" they were forced to sit through. He wondered why he'd given in so easily at the time, why he'd given up so quickly.

Vulnerabilities exist within the living hosts themselves. Licensed military personnel carry detectors to verify whether or not other personnel have removed their own chips. Removal of one's verification chip results in the forfeit of one's rank and is considered treason.

He left his hand inside his right pocket, scared to ever let go of what he'd held on to for so long now. Scared to lose it, unable to replicate it himself if it were ever destroyed.

New tissue-specific verification chips are expensive and cannot be mass produced due to the genetic materials needed during the initial production process.

He felt a sharp pain in the index finger of his right hand. A small cut, dripping fresh blood all over the contents he'd kept hidden.

Aside from the United States, no other political entity has any knowledge of the verification chips. Those involved in the engineering and implementation process were sworn by contract to remain silent on the chip's existence. In addition to the signed written contracts, individuals involved were implanted with a chip as well.

He knew he should've given it up the day he had first picked it up. His orders had been to destroy it, but he couldn't bring himself to say goodbye just yet.

If the chip were to be found by enemy lines, especially while still activated within the hosts, the data can be tracked and the technology reproduced if the resources and materials were available.

He watched the squared ceiling above, noticing all the bumpy imperfections of a sloppy paint job. The lights when on were too bright, reminded him of a hospital.

Not reporting a death or missing soldier, results in a high-risk state in which, when notified, all systems go into hibernation mode. Access codes must be entered in manually, given those few personnel with knowledge of the codes are in attendance.

He was grateful for the dark that the night brought on. He felt the stinging in his finger as he gripped the contents of his pocket tighter.

Lack of present authorized personnel results in a lockdown for all barracks until all verification chips are reset and those without a living host are deactivated.

Focusing on sleep he forced his eyes shut in an attempt to shut off his mind. The countless thoughts that brought a sickness into his stomach continued to breathe life into his fears and anxiety.

If for any reason, a verification chip is manufactured by sources preconceived as a threat, all chips go into countdown mode. At which time, all hosts must take measures to see medical personnel licensed in the removal of the chip. Failure to remove the verification chip results in termination of both the chip as well as the host. All digital records and documentation of biological and demographic information collected per personnel is destroyed.

Letting air slowly fill up his lungs then exhale, his mind went back to training. The briefs they'd had to listen to, the warnings resembling a broken record.

If the system is not notified of any outside threat to possession of the chip, all systems and processes continue as routinely identified.

He wondered why such precautions were taken; all security was meant to protect the soldiers and civilians and yet has the power to do just the opposite. Reality was funny in that way.

Military personnel—without the aid of systemized data and controls, will then deal with any consequences that are to incur as a result of the failure.

Chapter 8

That bitch he thought as he read through the letter. *That fucking cunt, now I have to give up an entire day for this shit.*

He'd received a subpoena to appear in court as one Alex Nessler's character witnesses. He hadn't seen her in over three years, what could he possibly have to say about her *character*?

There was plenty he recalled from his time together with her. He'd loved her and she turned out to be a selfish cunt, just leaving without an explanation, like he was nothing to her.

He hadn't bothered to find her, or demand any sort of explanation after that. He'd been too proud at the time. Besides, after he got over the initial feeling of abandonment and sadness any thought of her was soon consumed by anger. He simply didn't care enough to ever see or hear from her again.

Now, she's back in his life.

He heard about the murder from everywhere, on the news, in the paper, all over social media, he couldn't get away from it. Now, he *actually* has to take time out of his life to deal with this shit?

But poor Alex, there's no way she could've done it. No way she's guilty, she wouldn't have done it unless it was her only choice. There must be another explanation. Everyone they'd known was up and defending her, believing there's two sides to every story.

He knew better, she was a just a bitch. And whether or not that guy had it coming didn't make her any less so.

He remembered how she used to talk to other people; so

friendly and honest, everyone fucking loved her. No one ever questioned her almighty attitude. They really believed she was that much smarter, that much better than them.

He couldn't deny it, she was, still is. She gave off an aura of modesty and self -doubt, while at the front she was condescending and grim. No one ever questioned her, just wanted to know her and understand her. But there had been nothing to understand, she was miserable and no matter how much she acted otherwise and what she said her misery was contagious.

He'd ignored her strength, doubted her intelligence, and questioned her altruism. Good thing too, the bitch is a murderer. *Just sad*, he thought, *how I was the only one to see that.*

Sure, there had been moments when she was all he needed, for a time he couldn't picture his life without her. She'd made him better, he'd managed to briefly hold down a job, attend class almost everyday; he'd wanted to make her happy. Then she left and he gave up on all that. At the time it just didn't seem worth it.

Still wasn't. But now, while he was trying to move on with his life, he'd practically forgotten all about her—until now.

He wasn't entirely innocent during their time together. From the outside it may have appeared that she'd been the victim during the course of their relationship. But that's how Alex played it. It had always frustrated him. She'd drive him nuts with little comments here and there along with her ridiculous expectations of him. Then she'd push him to his boiling point. Yes, he was inconsiderate and flaky and would become completely unreasonable at times, but most of that had been her fault.

He read the court order over and over again. They didn't

get too detailed about the trial. But from what he can understand the prosecution was calling him in. He could be as honest as he wanted too, finally tell his side of the story, and ultimately let everyone know just who Alex Nessler really is.

The trial was set for two months from then. He had plenty of time to prepare. He wasn't going to be explicit during his testimony when it came to their relationship. He'd let them know just enough so it was clear that Alex wasn't as great as everyone had pegged her to be.

He thought about that date, another day gone to responsibility. And, it shouldn't even be his responsibility. He was getting frustrated just thinking about it. But deep down he didn't blame her. A small part of him, a part that he would never admit existed, not even acknowledged it to himself, made him just a little excited about the whole thing. *He was going to see Alex.* He smiled for a brief moment as the thought registered in his head.

Chapter 9

"Hey! Griff, wake up!" He felt someone shaking him, disturbing his dream. He couldn't remember when he'd fallen asleep. It had not come easily for him the night before. He continued to think of Alex and the chips. His thoughts, mostly aimless, kept him up; tossing and turning. He'd find a comfortable position, one arm underneath the cool pillow, his stomach facing the warmth of the bed, and before he knew it he was twisting again.

"Griffin, you're going to be late!" *Late for what?* He thought.

"GRIFFIN!" he realized it was Becks. Why was she so worked up for? He slowly began coming back to himself. Forcing himself awake though his body refused to give in, his eyes demanding otherwise.

He finally sat up, still groggy and his head was throbbing.

"Late for what?" he repeated the question, this time with voice.

"For work?"

"I'm not going in today, I can't." he gave in to his desire to return to bed. He'll deal with the consequences later. First he needed to get Becks off his case. And why was she even on it to begin with? The entire time she's been here, he hadn't seen her even lift a finger to help out. Right, she was on the run, sort of.

"Griffin, get up. You need to go to work." She was stubborn with this one.

"Becks..." he murmured. "I really can't. I haven't slept

right in days. I need some time to myself, some time to vent." He mustered up his most puppy dog voice as he said it. He meant most of it; he hadn't had a chance to tell Becks what was going on.

"Fine, go back to sleep. We'll talk later." She gave up more easily than he'd expected. Same as his mother always had when he refused to get up in the morning for class. He felt a pang of guilt as he made the resemblance.

"Thank you, don't be upset. I need you to understand."

"I'm not, I'll put the coffee on in an hour or so."

He'd fallen back asleep before she had finished her sentence. It was an easy sleep this time; no thoughts to hold him back from the REM he so desperately wanted. At times, he felt that these moments, those few moments where he can just let go and rest were better than any drug around. Yes, he loved his sleep, always had.

After what felt like only five minutes he heard Becks rummaging in the kitchen. He checked the time and realized it was late afternoon. He'd slept through the entire morning.

He quickly got up, throwing his blanket to the farthest corner of the bed. Slowly making his way into the kitchen, he forced himself to regain conscious, become more alert before talking to Becks.

He grabbed one of the cups she'd already filled up after hearing him approach. He drank it down greedily before lighting up a cigarette. His morning routine was always the same, no matter what time of day it actually was—coffee and a cigarette.

"Good morning sunshine" Becks said in a slightly condescending tone.

Geez what was her deal today? "Morning." He managed to grunt. Apparently he wasn't as alert as he'd hoped for. The headache was back, seemed to be getting worse. He poured himself another cup of coffee.

"What was it you needed to 'vent' about?" she was mocking him, he knew.

"Look Becks, I don't know why you're so…" he paused for a moment trying to find the correct word without offending her. The last thing he needed was a fight from her.

"So what?" her impatience annoyed him. He tried to hold it down.

"Nothing, I'm sorry if you're upset. That's all."

"I'm not upset Griffin, but you've been lounging around here for the past three days, aren't you worried about losing your job? Can you really keep taking so much time off consecutively?"

Three days, what the hell.

"I'm sorry Griffin, I don't know what kind of mood you're in or what put you in it, but this is a bit ridiculous."

That's right. He'd gotten home late after his last shift, needed something to take the edge off. He saw her bottle of oxycodone, favorite comedown antidote and just went for it. *Was that really three days ago?* He thought about it for a second and realized that he hadn't left his bedroom aside from the occasional piss trip, hadn't even eaten anything, just kept popping pills and passing out over and over again.

"So, do you want to tell me what the hell is going on?" she demanded.

"Yes, I will. I just need to take a shower first or something." He really needed to wake up, lose the fog that surrounded him.

He downed his second cup and made his way into the bathroom. Closing the door behind him, the room quickly filled up with steam.

Stripping off his boxers he got in and let the hot water fall over him. God, it felt so good. His head was still pounding but the cascading water made it bearable.

"Griffin! What are you doing in there?" she sounded worried.

He jerked awake, realized he'd fallen asleep in the shower. His hands had taken on the familiar prune texture. How long had he been in there? He wondered, an hour? Maybe more?

"Yea" he called back, "I'll be right out." He yelled louder this time before turning off the shower.

Chapter 10

The courtroom was frenzied by the time he got there. Witnesses, family members, reporters, everyone was there, trying to settle in. The defense attorney noticed him as he entered the room. He was tall, handsome, yet his face gave him away. The guy was frustrated, actively trying to work something out.

"Mr. Scoarse? I'm Kirk Michaels, the attorney assigned to Miss Nessler's case." He reached out his right hand.

"Yes?" Griffin accepted the handshake, noticing the grip.

"Thank you for coming in today, but you must have not received the update."

"What update?"

"You will not be called to the stand today, though we appreciate your being in attendance today Mr. Scoarse."

"Why not?" Griffin was a little relieved, but confused at the news.

"For legal reasons, neither the persecution nor myself will require any additional character witnesses at this time. But you are welcome to stay with the audience to watch over the proceedings." With that he turned his back to Griffin and walked briskly back to Alex's side.

Taking a seat on the bench towards the back of the courtroom Griffin wondered why his testimony wasn't of any importance to Alex's case. Though he no longer had to speak, he sensed that familiar feeling that he'd always endured when around Alex. He suddenly felt abandoned, irrelevant to her.

The judge finally showed up about a half hour later. The

room fell silent. Alex was then led out, she was wearing the typical light blue jumpsuit and her hands were cuffed behind her back. They directed her by her elbow towards the left side of the room where she sat beside a tall, light skinned man. He looked no older than thirty years old, dressed to the T in his darkest suit—the ultimate all American lawyer.

They removed her handcuffs and the trial began. The prosecution and defense attorneys introduced their case and finally it was time for the witnesses to take the stand.

They first led out a young girl, maybe fifteen. She had been one of the victims of the man Alex had murdered.

They went back and forth with her for some time. The defense really playing up the horrors this young girl had gone through from having been raped.

By the time she was done talking, everyone looked toward Alex as a hero. *Fuck, everyone always loves her, she can do no wrong* he thought as the prosecution called forth their first character witness. Some guy named Dylan.

He was on the skinny side, taller than Griffin. Feeling jealousy build up inside of him he tried to pay attention to what the guy had to say.

He knew Alex after their relationship had ended. He'd slept with her, had his own relationship with her, *did she really refer to this guy as her boyfriend?*

He listened attentively as Dylan spoke. Recounting his time together with her. Most of what he said was on point with everything Griffin had been planning. Only Dylan was far angrier with her, didn't seem to care what happened to her at all.

She really fucked this guy up. How many other guys did she date after me? How many had she slept with?

He tried not to think about that. He focused hard on

keeping his composure together; they would call him to the stand at any moment now.

Dylan continued to speak for about an hour as he was cross-examined by the attorneys. He got more and more emotional as the questioning progressed, pegging Alex as some evil demon bitch.

He stared at Alex's back, couldn't see her face from where he sat. He wondered if her face would reveal any emotion. From behind she didn't move a muscle, just focused on what was straight ahead of her. It seemed as is she was in her own world, zoning out. Looking in Dylan's direction but not really watching him, instead she appeared to be staring right through him.

Would she have any emotion when I take the stand?

He put his focus back on Dylan. "She's a sociopath, she has absolutely no conscience, no guilt or remorse for her actions" Dylan continued. *He must've watched way too much "Law and Order"* thought Griffin.

Not long after Dylan's testimony was over, Alex had been called to the stand.

Even after all those years, she was still beautiful, still the same old Alex. She sat facing him, her eyes briefly scanning the room as they locked in on his.

He held her gaze for what felt like ages, completely forgetting how he'd felt only moments earlier. He missed her; missed their life together, missed the way she used to laugh and how, no matter what happened during the day, the highlight had always been going to bed with her. Knowing she was there, right by his side, he missed all of that.

She began to speak. Her voice was different somehow, monotone. Not the way she usually spoke. He realized she was putting on an act, trying to make the jury uncomfortable.

Why is she doing that? They were on her side, why is she ruining it?

She continued to speak in that same manner; she came off insane, cruel.

They don't need me. He realized.

She met his gaze again, by accident it seemed. She suddenly stopped talking forgetting what to say next as she stared at him. Then, she quickly composed herself and gave off a slightly nervous laugh, coming off as a simple young girl not the monster she had been trying to paint.

Before anyone can change his or her mind about her, she returned to that monotone voice.

Once the testimony was over and the attorneys gave their closing arguments, the jury left the room.

After only a couple hours they retuned with the verdict.

He knew what it was before they said it, "Guilty."

The guards began to lead her away after the sentencing was announced. As she walked out, he hoped she'd look his way, one more time.

She hadn't.

That was the last time he'd seen her alive.

PART FOUR

Chapter 1

The light was blinking on and off, almost as if the bulb was about to go out. A faulty electric line, briefly lighting up the dank, gray room.

He slowly regained consciousness, unsure of where he was. He felt a stab of pain in his gut as he eyes slowly adjusted to the dimly lit room. He could hear voices nearby.

As his vision came into focus, he noticed the ceiling above was entirely mirrored. He could see his reflection.

He tried to get up, realizing he couldn't move his body. He focused on the muscles of his legs, willing them to move but nothing happened. He tried to lift his arms up but couldn't gain control of his movements. He felt strapped down but didn't feel any straps around him. He was lying on a metal gurney in the middle of the room with one light fixture towards the entrance of the room.

He strained to move his neck, in the direction of the voices, but could not force any movement.

He looked up; saw himself lying on the gurney. He was naked.

"What's going on?" he asked no one in particular.

Panic began to set in when he noticed a small metallic medical table in the reflection from above. There were scalpels, saws, syringes, all rusted with what appeared to be dried blood. Slowly it has begun to dawn on him, his paralysis, the missing prisoners...

"HELP!" he screamed. He continued to scream for several minutes when the voices finally stopped.

The door to the room slowly creaked open and he could hear the thump of footsteps approaching toward him.

From the mirror above he can see three men entering through the open doorway. Two dressed as soldiers, one in a lab coat.

The third appeared to be some kind of doctor or surgeon. He had large brown and red stains running down the front of the white coat. He slowly realized those stains were blood, some set in with what appeared to have been an attempt to wash them out. Others, however, were fresh. The blood still hadn't dried in several spots. Random red splatters stung the coat, glistening with moisture.

"Is he fully paralyzed?" one of the soldiers asked ."Yes" he replied nonchalantly.

"When can you start on this one?"

"Right away," the doctor responded, heading over to the small medical table.

He glanced in the mirror above, watching as the doctor began sorting through the medical equipment. It was almost as if he wasn't sure which to pick up, or weighing his options.

"What the hell is going on?" he asked. "Why am I here? What are you planning to do?" his voice became more hoarse as he continued. It was becoming difficult to speak. He suddenly felt weak, exhausted.

The three men simply ignored him. The doctor made his way back with a small scalpel in his hand.

"Are we to remove the device first?" he asked the soldier.

"No, let's see if it disarms due to his body heat or if it can read his brain signals"

"As you wish."

The doctor walked over to the gurney, putting on a facemask as he did so.

He watched with horror through the mirror above, with horror as the doctor lifted up the scalpel, bringing it down to his abdomen. He couldn't feel the cold steel of the knife as it sliced through him, but his body sent pain signals to his brain.

The slices were unbearable, as the cuts became deeper and deeper, cutting through flesh and muscle, he couldn't hold back anymore. He began screaming out, closing his eyes shut, tears welling up and running down the sides of his face.

"He's not watching" the first soldier noted.

The doctor stopped what he was doing. Cleaned off the scalpel by wiping it on one sleeve.

In the reflection he could see pools of his blood slowly forming around his body, dripping to the floor as it ran down towards a drain in the center of the old tile floor.

He could feel someone grab his head. "Get off me, get the fuck off me!" He started screaming again.

It was the doctor; he placed his head perfectly to the center and peered down at him. He could see a smirk on his face, his eyes dancing with satisfaction as he tapped his eyelids to his brows, forcing his eyes to remain open.

Grabbing a syringe from inside his coat pocket, the doctor stuck it inside his mouth. Piercing his tongue and cheeks, completely paralyzing him now.

He tried to speak but could not.

All he could do now is stare up, watch everything in the reflection above.

"Let's continue" the second soldier finally spoke, he wanted to get it over with, his patience was running out.

"Of course" the doctor walked back over to his operating position over the abdomen, slowly piercing the flesh once more.

Chapter 2

"Where the hell have you been Scoarse?" the commanding officer demanded.

"I was sick"

"Sick? How fucking sick? You cannot disappear, no word, people have lost their jobs over less."

"I'm sorry sir, it won't happen again."

This was enough for Brinks, as he nodded "Get to work."

Though Griffin wasn't aware of it, his leaving or being fired was a security risk. The officers knew this, realized he may know too much of what was happening.

"Yes sir" Griffin replied politely.

He slumped over to the kitchen; it was time to prepare breakfast... again.

His morning duties went by quicker than he thought it would. It had been noon in what felt like a blink of an eye. The day was moving fast. He knew a good rest would help him out.

He was surprised they hadn't given him too much shit for it. Relieved that he still had a job to return to. *Becks had been worried for no reason.*

He was let into the dormitory on the farthest right corner of the barracks. He was to start the weekly clear-out here. He began stripping off the bed sheets and pillowcases from each of the bunks.

New soldiers came and went to the barracks, each week those who were released from the infirmary and were in healthy condition were to go back to the frontlines. Finish their duty to their country.

It was a routine, one that never ended. Go off to war, fight, come back and regain your strength for a brief moment of time before going out again. Unless you died, the cycle would continue.

Griffin thought of Lynns and Bryans, wondering what else they'd knew of Alex, of what kind of person she'd become, if she'd been happy. Then his thoughts went elsewhere, there was something they weren't telling them.

He remembered their secret conversation in the cafeteria earlier that week. They were definitely hiding something, whatever it was they seemed to be frightened of it.

Maybe he'll sneak in some liquor for Lynns, he seemed willing to have a good time. Just a couple guys having a drink in the middle of the night. That was the only way he could get them to talk.

He heard the dormitory door open behind him. It was Bryans.

"Sorry, didn't realize you were in here" startled when he saw Griffin.

"That's alright, need me to leave?"

"No, no that's alright, I'll come back later." He quickly left, shutting the door behind him.

After he'd left Griffin realized that this wasn't the dormitory Bryans was authorized for. His wouldn't be cleared out for a few more days.

Why was he in here? Better yet, how did he gain access to this room? Griffin wondered, before shrugging it off.

Chapter 3

He had been a respected member of the community before the war had begun. Top in his class when he'd completed his medical training and residency. He'd had a wife and two beautiful blonde blue eyed daughters. He was an ordinary man, with a successful career, and a loving family. No one would have ever guessed where he'd end up; his neighbors in the North Carolina suburbs would never have even fathomed it.

He lost his family during the second bombing. He'd had it all and in a blink of an eye lost everything. From then on, he'd blamed the government more so than any enemy his country would possess. He'd blamed them for not having done anything to defend the citizens of the nation, for not having been able to defend the lives of his family, to not have protected his livelihood.

The lights continued to dim as he operated on the nameless soldier before him. He'd never realized when he first began that he would learn to enjoy it all so much. For the first time since his life as a respected surgeon, caring father and husband had ended; he'd finally had something to look forward to.

He monitored the soldier's heart rate, as he continued to cut into his flesh, muscle, and guts. He imagined what it might be like to be him. Lying on a cold gurney, unable to move or speak. Being forced to watch as his body was mutilated.

It was that last part that had been his idea. He wanted others to see his work, including the subjects. He needed them to know his skill, his talents, what he'd worked so hard to become.

He did not regret any of it. His philosophy had always been that everything happened for a reason. No matter the misery he'd had to go through and the pain he was forced to overcome, it had all led up to this. He'd convinced himself that he was doing this for research, for his career, and most importantly, personal fulfillment.

He would never call it torture, though torture it was. His love for the suffering of others overtook him on a daily basis. He enjoyed nothing more than having them watch as he slowly drained them of any life. This had become his personal revenge. He enjoyed every second of it.

He knew that if society would ever return, if everything would go back to normal, whatever normal actually meant, he would lose his medical license—be shunned by the community. They'd probably convict him on various war crime charges. But, that would never happen. *This* is normal now, *this* is society.

He looked down at the soldier. Saw the bleak tears spilling down the sides of his face, unable to look away from what was happening to him.

On days like these, he made an effort to make conversation with his subjects. They deserved some social break, especially if it meant that his voice would be the last thing that they'd ever hear.

"I bet you're wondering about your pretty friend." He began, his voice sinister. Yes, he enjoyed this part very much.

He moved towards the soldier's wrist. They didn't have much time. His rate was slowing, body temperature dropping.

"It was brave of you to volunteer in her place" he continued as he sliced into the wrist, careful to not damage the chip.

"But, you would've ended up on my table anyway…" he remained focused on the chip, slowly peeling away the skin to reveal the metal underneath.

"Well, as for her…" he chose his words carefully. Noticing on the monitor that the soldier's heart rate was increasing. A good sign. He had more time. This one was stronger than the others.

"Let's just say that you took her place after all…"

Chapter 4

He missed the train back by only a few seconds. Another won't arrive for a couple more hours. He hated nights like these. Cold, quiet nights, alone on the platform waiting for a train that would never come.

Far too often his mind got the better of him. Anything to escape the cold, he desperately focused on other thoughts, often times creating scenarios that never existed prior. This particular night was colder than usual. There was no one else on the platform with him. It was two in the morning and what should only be an hour-long ride had just turned into three.

He spent more time waiting for the train than actually riding it. The commute in the morning was rarely this horrendous, at least then he had control of the timing, when he left his apartment to catch the next arrival.

Work had not been kind to him either, not today. His hands reeked of vinegar, bleach and piss. He couldn't wait to get home, and wash it all away. Becks would probably be asleep by the time he'd make it back, they will have to talk another time.

In the meantime, he tucked his frozen hands deep inside his pockets, searching for any warmth where there was none. He let go of his surroundings and began rethinking the day's events.

He had been certain that the two soldiers, Bryans and Lynns, were up to something. Certain that they were hiding something.

They know more than they're letting on, about what had

happened during the attack on the camp and what had become of Alex.

What had they been whispering about in the cafeteria last week? He wished he had been able to focus more on their conversation, but the two were inaudible. Especially amongst the clanking of dirty pots and trays.

He wondered why they had been so quick to end their conversation with him when the chip had been brought up. There was something they were hiding, something about Alex and her designated chip.

It bothered him that he was so quick to let Bryans leave the dormitory earlier today. There was no reason for him to have been in there, especially without any granted access. Those two were up to something, he just couldn't figure out what.

He needed to talk to someone, explain all the questions. He needed Becks. She was the only other person who would listen to him, besides the voice in his head.

She'd bring him back down to reality, explain everything. The paranoia was getting to be too much for him. Maybe he really was overthinking things, maybe Bryans did have authorization to enter that dormitory.

Once again, he went on another rant. Another conspiracy theory. Those men fought alongside Alex, they had not done anything wrong besides survive.

Is that what he was blaming them for? Surviving?

He felt guilty at the idea. *They were soldiers, loyal to their country; they wouldn't do anything to harm our welfare, would they?*

They came in fatigued, traumatized. Whatever had happened over in Alaska must have been quite an ordeal. They weren't hiding anything, weren't plotting against national security. By the time the train had finally arrived, he'd convinced himself that there was nothing to worry about. He was simply being paranoid, putting blame where there shouldn't be any.

They are good men he reassured himself. *They did everything they could for her.*

Chapter 5

"Bryans, you need to start moving, get a head start." She whispered.

He watched her as he hesitated, *what was she up to?*

His leg was burning from the inside, from where they had excavated the bullet. He tried to get up, to hold his own, and quickly fell back down.

He knew if he wanted to survive, he'd have to follow her orders. Funny how she was the one giving orders now. The only one who was able to keep a cool head amidst all the turmoil.

He knew the enemy was approaching, knew that he'd have to make a break for it soon. But, he couldn't leave Nessler and Lynns behind.

He watched as his blood tainted the freshly fallen snow. Looking up he saw her biting down on the long side of her belt, she'd taken it off and wrapped it around her forearm. Picking up her knife she jaggedly cut through the skin of her wrist, not going too deep but deep enough to leave sprinkles of blood right underneath. She stifled her screams as she bit down and dug out the metal chip.

He understood what she was doing, what she was planning. She knew there was a chance she wouldn't make it out alive, taking precaution in case the worst did happen.

"No... I can't leave you behind." He told her, trying to sound confident, failing in doing so as his voice hesitated and cracked.

She threw the chip towards him as she spoke. He could

faintly hear her explaining what her next move was. "But I *need* you to watch my back." He listened as he picked up her chip, watched the dim red light slowly blinking to her heart beat. It would take several more minutes for the chip to lose some power, without any body heat, most of the chips would go into hibernation, before being exposed to heat once again, human heat.

He stowed her chip safely away inside one of his pockets before zipping it closed. When he heard her scream, ordering him to go, he forced himself to get up. To ignore the sharp stabs of pain shooting up and down his leg as he ran.

****

He woke up surrounded by a pool of his own sweat. He couldn't see Lynns in the dark but was able to hear his minute wheezing as he slept. He knew Lynns would be re-envisioning everything from that day as well. Best not to bother him just yet.

He stayed in bed, moved the cheap polyester blanket down towards his waist. He was getting tired of having to relive that attack over and over again.

He knew Lynns was guilty for what had happened, he wasn't innocent either. He could've talked her out of it, could've stayed behind and helped instead of running like a little coward. Yes, those had been her orders, but she was not his commander. He was hers.

He should have been there for her, injured or not. In a moment of weakness, he'd forgotten what was his role had been, forgotten that they were his responsibility and not vice versa.

Staring up at the dark ceiling he reached into his pocket.

Her chip was still there. He knew he should have informed the others, should have reported it and returned it. Or, at the very least, destroyed it.

Lynns argued with him earlier on the matter. Scared he'd get caught with it. How would he be able to explain it then?

He wouldn't.

He fingered the chip for a bit, running his forefinger up and down its sharp edges before bringing it up to his focal point.

The light was dimmer now, not as strong as it had been when she had first removed it.

He had one just like it inside his own wrist and wondered just how long it would take before all their chips were set to self-destruct.

He knew it was a risk holding on to hers, but he was certain he'd disarmed it. As far the computer knew, the chip he now held belonged to an anonymous soldier, a John Doe in the system. At least he'd hoped that was the case.

So far it was working. Unless Alex was authorized to get in anywhere at anytime, he was sure he'd reset it.

Lynns wasn't too happy about this recent accomplishment. But he knew Lynns wouldn't talk. Knew that the chip was still his for the time being.

There was still much more he could manipulate, he only needed more time...

Chapter 6

He jerked awake hitting his head against the metal railing connected from the top of the train to the pale dark purple seats. He'd fallen asleep. Barely missing his stop.

He quickly got off before the doors shut and the train moved on to its next destination. It was still dark out when he made it out onto the street. He could see his breath ahead of him as he walked. The night had gotten colder.

He walked quickly back to his apartment, lighting a cigarette to keep him company as he did so. The cold kept him awake as he approached his building. He'd b able to get maybe a couple more hours of sleep in if he was lucky.

"Hey Griff"

He was surprised to find her still awake as he opened the door to the apartment. She was sitting by the kitchen table, cradling a mug of tea.

"Why are you up?"

"I couldn't sleep, decided to wait up for you. How was work? Did you miss the train again?"

"Yea...work was fine..." he hesitated as he tried to decide whether or not he should tell her of his conspiracy theories. If anything, maybe she'll reassure him that he's just being paranoid, looking for drama where there is none.

"I wanted to run something past you, get your opinion on –
"

He suddenly stopped when he noticed her puffy eyes and runny nose.

"Becks..." he approached her "What's wrong?"

He asked out of courtesy, feeling instantly more tired as he placed his hand on her shoulder.

"I don't know Griff, I keep having this dream. I sit there. Just sit, in the old barn. The wooden walls are rotting away around me and all I can smell is horse shit."

He made an effort to stay up, to listen to her.

"Sitting on one lonely little chair in the middle of the barn, I slice my arms over and over again, and watch the blood drain out, slowly...patiently."

He poured himself a cup of coffee and lit another cigarette as she went on.

"I watch the blood pool up all around me. Thinking, this is it, it can all finally end. But it never works out like that. Just as soon as I feel that beautiful numbness, that relieving form of release, I realize I can open my eyes. And I'm forced to watch with despair and disappointment as the blood defies gravity. Floating off the floor, refilling my recently emptied, just freed veins. I continue to watch as the wounds on my skin, all along my arms, are sealed up, all in an instant, like it never even happened...and I wonder every time...if it's ever going to end."

He stubbed out his cigarette and just stared at her, unsure of what to say or how to act. He wanted so desperately to just go in his bedroom, close the door, hug his cool pillow and fall asleep.

"I'm sorry" she got up and went towards the sink, turning it on to wash out her mug.

She didn't expect him to respond, all she'd needed was someone to talk to.

He realized that they had all lost their lives, no matter who you were all those years ago, if you were still alive you were no longer that same person.

She was no exception.

And now, all she wanted was a way out. This wasn't life. They both knew that.

"Let's try to get some sleep, some rest." Was all he could muster.

She nodded as they went inside his bedroom and shut the door.

Chapter 7

He thought back to the first day she had been thrown into the cell he'd shared with two others prior. They'd kept a bag over her head as they shoved her in and locked the steel bar door behind them.

He was beginning to feel numb all over, the pain was no longer there. He could no longer feel any of it. He continued to think back, back to what might have happened to her. He fought hard too make sure she would stay alive. Every time they escorted someone out of cell, they never returned.

They weren't fed for several days, but water had been provided to them. It was murky and slightly stank of sulfur, but they greedily drank it down every time the bucket arrived.

He'd been forced to watch them beat and rape her, over and over again, day after day. Usually they'd get all their energy out on her before they turned on him. Beating him and pissing on him. Her cowering in her usual corner of the cell.

Each time they left, she'd huddle in a corner and quietly weep to herself.

He hadn't spoken to her much, neither one of them was up for any conversation. But she was strong, she took everything they threw at her. He'd noticed her wrist was bandaged up with what appeared to be a piece of her shirt. She must've removed her chip.

He looked around for anything he could use to remove and destroy his own. There was nothing in the cell but her and the water bucket along with additional buckets filled with their waste—urine and feces molding away.

After one particular nasty encounter he knew she couldn't take any more. This time, they seemed to not have any energy to waste on him.

Struggling to pull her stained clothing back on, he walked over to her and just held her.

They sat like that for hours, crying together, for themselves, for each other, for everything. No words were spoken, they were unnecessary.

They must've stayed that way all night, only torn apart by the men who reentered the cell as the small light of day bleakly shown through the small window above.

Once again, they'd gone after her. Pulling him off of her and throwing him against the brick and cement wall across the cell. He remembered bashing his head, remembered anger taking over.

They were human beings, not cattle. *This was not going to be the way this ends.*

That thought kept him fighting, gave him the strength to defend her. He attacked one of the men from behind, grasping his elbow around his neck and pushing as hard as he could. Before he knew it he was on the ground again.

One of the others knocked him over the head—hard this time. He continued to beat him until all he saw was blood and mucus around him. His vision slowly lost focus, and he passed out.

Only to wake up on the operating table of horror.

He could see his chip had been removed, along with his entire forearm—from the elbow to the wrist.

He could see his dismembered hand lying at his side, attached to nothing but the blood oozing out of it.

The doctor continued to talk, to talk of the girl he'd tried to help.

"You see, she died very much the same as you. Only she had not given me any particular pleasure personally. You on the other hand, well, thanks for the hand" the doctor chuckled.

He no longer cared enough to fight. It felt good to let go. To give in and just let go.

Chapter 8

"Growing up we never thought it would end with us. Our generation, they called us the 'me' gen, we never imagined there'd ever be this serious of a war, *I mean it's the fucking end of the world.* That *kind of war.*

"In school you learn about the civil war, the world wars, and every time you think; 'that won't be me. It won't happen during *my* life time.' But it had…slowly it had. There was Afghanistan, when we were just kids, then Iraq, the conflict in Israel, then the Ukraine and the Soviets., fucking ISIS. But we were still in denial, somehow we refused to below that any of it would ever truly affect us.

"They taught us all about the ozone layer, global warming, the depletion of natural resources. Along with the unbalanced, unsustainable environmental yield. Lectures were centered on mankind, on how man had singlehandedly destroyed entire ecosystems, how we've led several species to extinction.

"They teach you of the chemicals and processed foods we consume, of our high consumption rates. And yet we still refused to see it coming…

"Of all past generations, after everything, it was all leading up to this. The exponential growth of technological evolution, of the capabilities we had instilled in everyday devices. Devices we couldn't go a day without. All the signs were there. We just refused to see them. And we'd be the ones to have to deal with it, to clean up the mess. Only we couldn't. Still can't.

"Our spoiled nature, our delusions keep us from moving

forward. Instead we fight, fight ourselves to our own extinction.

"The whole world is at war, and yet we're still in denial…"

He sat silent for a moment, staring out the window. It was snowing outside. It had been one of the coldest winters yet. He felt a small shiver trail down his back. *This will never end* he thought.

"Corporal, do you really think everyone is left in denial? All those men and women out there? Or is it just you?"

She was pretty, maybe only a couple years younger than him. He wondered how there could still be doctors around, psychiatrists for that matter. But this was her job, *yes, even you're in denial doc.*

"No, it's not just me. Look around; we're encased in this small room with just one little window. Guarded on all sides. You're in the fucking barracks for fucks sake pretending that any of this is in any way normal."

"Maybe Corporal. Maybe I'm pretending that this room can be a good excuse for an office. Maybe I go home every night thinking that my shift is over and sit down with my steak dinner with a full glass of red wine. Maybe I wake up every morning fearing that bombs will rain down any second now. But, maybe that is normal. This is our world now, and either we accept it or we fight it."

"Fight, yes. Is that what you think I'm doing? Fighting the reality of our situation?" Bryans asked.

"Are you?"

He hated when they did that. All those shrinks, always the same. He came in looking for answers, for help, not having his questions thrown back at him.

"All I know is, everything's changed, everything just feels wrong."

"Why do you say that?"

"When I was studying, back in MIT all those years ago, I think back and it just feels like a different lifetime."

"What did you study Corporal?"

"Computer engineering. I was a geek back then. Made my parents proud. I loved it, loved the programming, the wiring, the coding, the architecture...I still love it."

He felt the edge of the chip in his pocket as he spoke, slowly smiling. *Maybe there was something to look forward to.*

"Why did you choose to go into combat then? Why not work for the military using your skills?"

"I had to fight. I was drafted. I didn't see a purpose to showing off my *skill set.* I was still a student at the time when the notice came in. I wasn't good enough, still not good enough."

"Did you always doubt your capabilities?"

"No, I'm just being honest. I'm no Einstein, definitely not the next Gates..." he pulled his hand out of his pocket, away from the chip.

"That may be true Jason. But you didn't have to give up. You must've know that. Tell more about what happened over in Alaska. What happened with Alex?"

It always goes back to her.

"Like I said before, she died. There was nothing we could've done. She gave her life for us. For that, I'm grateful. But what kind of life is this anyway? Maybe she did herself a favor in the end."

"Do you feel guilty?"

"Of course I feel guilty. She was a friend, a good soldier. I was responsible for her."

"But there was nothing you could've done in this situation, as you said earlier, those were the cards you were dealt."

"Yes, she died so that we could survive.

Chapter 9

"Can we proceed Dr. Rechter?" asked one of the men as he entered the surgical room.

"Yes, but you would need to be careful. From the heart monitors and the rate of the chip's signal, I would advise against implantation at this particular moment." Dr. Rechter said as he scrubbed off his surgical tools.

He was suddenly tired, the clean up was not something he looked forward to after a day of precision on the operating table.

"Why Doctor?"

"From what I've witnessed, the chips are at their best when inside a human host, they begin to slowly die out without human heat to keep them charged. Whether the host is living, in pain, or dead the chip is not affected. As long as the body is sustained at a certain temperature, regular body heat."

"So what's the problem?" Impatience getting the best of him. He needed to have something positive to report. They didn't have much time. After years of planning, they were finally getting somewhere; their plan of attack couldn't wait much longer.

"I'm not an engineer Tim, you'd need to find someone who specializes in this technology. The chip needs to be reprogrammed, to a John Doe. It will not react safely within a new host. Each chip is similar to a barcode: one of a kind. At least from what I've noticed. Inserting Soldier A's chip into Soldier B may result in detonation. I'm only taking precaution."

Tim analyzed the situation carefully. They had the chips they needed and the new hosts. What the doctor wasn't aware of were the others involved, they already knew this.

"We can deal with the technological aspect. How quickly can you get the implants done?"

"First thing tomorrow morning if the men are ready."

"Perfect." Tim smiled as he left the room and headed towards the office, he had good news to report after all.

"Phil, they can go into surgery tomorrow."

"Great Tim, have they received the blueprints? We need to make sure they're ready."

"Yes, of course. They know the barracks in and out. Were we able to decentralize the chips?"

"They are done. Only need a new body suit."

"Very well then, they should be shipped out within a couple days. The men are ready."

"We'll need to regroup before then. This is a one shot deal. If we fail the first time, there won't be a second. This may just be our only way in."

"I am aware sir. I've trained them myself. All communications are to be severed as soon as G47 goes off."

"No loose ends?"

"None. There won't be. They have their scripts, know exactly what to say and what to expect. From the reports we've found in the abandoned barracks I was able to take note. They will go through a health screening upon initial arrival. A short interview will be conducted as well. The officials in the barracks will treat them like any other American soldier. They don't have a log of names and faces at hand, it seems they don't seem to bother with records much. The chip is all the precaution and authorization they will need."

"Excellent Tim. Will you be joining them for this round?"

"Of course Sir."

"Good, remember, no loose ends."

" I understand Sir."

Chapter 10

He arrived to the Barracks earlier than he wanted. Having been unable to sleep the night before he'd gotten up early to get dressed. He was beginning to regret that decision now.

Becks had been sound asleep when he'd left, hadn't even stirred while he was getting ready. He envied her for that; envied her for still being in bed and never having to actually go anywhere.

He stepped out for a smoke to kill some time. He watched as the smoke he exhaled became more concentrated as his breath hit the cold air. To warm up he distracted himself from the cold by walking around a little. He walked down several blocks, the fingers of his right hand already starting to ache from the cold when he noticed the church at the end of the corner.

The roof was a pointed dome, with the protestant cross at the very top. The closer he came the more apparent it was that the church had not been in service for quite some time. The red bricks were covered in senseless graffiti and the walkway was overgrown with weeds.

He walked up the crumbling steps, surprised to find the door unlocked. It squeaked loudly as he slowly opened the wooden entranceway. As he allowed himself inside, he realized he was completely alone.

The church smelt of damp mold and rotten wood. The candles around images of the various disciples were unlit, unevenly coated in used wax running down the sides. The pews were dusty and only the light from the blurred dirty windows illuminated the area, making the dust that much more visible. There would no longer be any solace.

He suddenly felt for the gold chain and cross around his neck, wearing it only because his mother had insisted all those years ago, now it had become a habit. He was half taken aback to find it still hanging around his neck, same spot as always. It'd been years since he'd given it any thought.

He wasn't the religious type, not even remotely. And who would be in today's world? He had at one time wanted to believe that there was something, anything out there…that life had a deeper meaning. But that was a long time ago. Religion he soon realized was only a coping method for believers and a way to maintain order for the enforcers. A man-made lie he no longer chose to be ignorant of.

He left the church just as quickly as he'd initially entered it and made his way back to the barracks. The sun was brighter now, the snow slowly beginning to melt along the sidewalks. He lit another cigarette for the company.

By the time he made it back the soldiers were already awake. He was late to his kitchen duties and quickly changed into the mandatory apron and plastic gloves. Before he'd made it past the double swinging doors to the large pots waiting for him, commander Brinks accompanied by the Sergeant approached him.

He rarely spoke to the Sergeant; an officer of higher ranking was above any nameless cook and janitor. He was tall, and built for his height, demanding respect from his intimidating appearance.

"We have an unexpected arrival. You'll need to get your ass over to the infirmary and clean up the place as soon as possible. Breakfast will be a few minutes late today." Brinks ordered.

"Yes sir" he responded as he proceeded towards the infirmary. He knew the soldiers wouldn't be too happy with their bland breakfast coming so late in the day. Hopefully they won't take it out on him.

Upon entering the nurses' station he was welcomed by three new men. He'd never seen them before, *new soldiers finally arriving home* he thought.

They were unshaven and looked hostile. Then again most of the returning soldiers usually presented themselves in the same fashion.

There were three of them. He'd always hated multiples of three, gave him an unsteady feeling. The whole pretense of a third wheel—where one truly didn't belong.

PART FIVE

Chapter 1

"Names and ranking please" the nurse asked of the new arrivals.

"I'm Jim Ticker, Private. This is Jackson Greenburg, Private" he said pointing to the soldier at his right "And he's Fred Hash, also Private" he motioned to the third soldier.

Griffin found it odd that of the three only one spoke for all of them. The three looked disheveled, their uniforms were ill fitting and soiled, facial hair completely overgrown. If it weren't for Tinker's voice and lack of an accent, he would've never pegged them for American soldiers.

"All privates? Where is your corporal?" the sergeant asked.

"He died in the field," again, only Ticker answered.

"Where was your company?"

"Alaska."

"Why haven't we been informed of your arrival?"

"We should be in the records" Ticker went on. "We've been out there since the initial draft, fighting for a long time. Our communications were cut off shortly after deployment. Haven't had the chance to return, we were stuck out there. That could be why."

The sergeant nodded, seeming content with the answer.

"Let's get you all checked out," the nurse said smiling.

This was his cue to head toward the dormitories. Time to clean out a new room and replace the sheets for the new soldiers.

As he walked out he noticed Bryans listening in, not making any attempt to pretend otherwise.

"You shouldn't be here"

Startled, Bryans simply stared at him for half a minute before responding.

"Something's not right with those three" he told Griffin.

"What do you mean?"

"Look at them. They have no serious injuries. They're not talking like soldiers, something's off about their tone. I haven't heard them give their corporal's name or any explanation as to what happened to the rest of their company. They don't seem to be too upset about anything or even relieved to be out of the field...Plus, the whole situation's odd...we were out in Alaska too, Lynns and I...something about them seems familiar but I'm certain we've never met them. Never crossed peaceful paths..." he trailed off.

Griffin needed to get the bunks cleared out and replaced. There was also the business of breakfast, which he had yet to get to. He didn't have time to listen to Bryans' theories.

"You're just being paranoid—"

"Yes, maybe" Bryans cut him off. "It just doesn't match up. I don't think we should be so quick to welcome them into the Barracks. Everything is off about this whole arrival. No one informed the Sergeant or Brinks that they were coming; they somehow lost communications early on with the base and never made an attempt, after all those years, to regain them. You're right though, maybe I am just being paranoid, this is a safe place after all, at least for the time being—"

"I really have to go, you should too. Don't let the Sergeant see you here."

"Of course..."

Griffin made his way out, before turning towards the dormitories he heard Bryans whisper to himself.

"But why are their left wrists fresh from surgery..."

Chapter 2

"Anything bothering you, Bryans?"

"Why do you ask?"

"You seem...closed off. Something's on your mind. Let me help you."

"It's nothing. I've just been thinking about the new arrivals from the other day."

"Why does that bother you?"

"Not really sure, I just have a strange feeling about them."

"Why do you say that?"

"They...just don't seem like soldiers...I don't know. I don't trust them."

"Have you voiced your concerns to anyone else?"

"Not really, well one other person. A member of the staff."

"Do you know the name?"

"He's the stumpy short one...always around..."

"Does Griffin Scoarse sound familiar?"

"Yes...I believe that's him... Have you spoken to any of them, the 'soldiers' since they've arrived?"

"Yes, we've gone through the preliminary examination. But I cannot tell you more, the whole doctor patient confidentiality."

"I understand"

"I cannot tell you what is said in here behind closed doors, I do the same courtesy for you. However, if you happen to hear something...that is beyond my control."

He wondered what she was implying. He couldn't be the only one to sense that something was off with them.

145

"I understand" he repeated.

"You'll be deployed soon, how are you feeling about that?"

"Not sure doc. I guess…uneasy."

"Uneasy?"

"Yes, I mean I barely got out alive last time."

"Are you prepared?"

He thought about that for a while. Physically, his leg was almost fully healed. He'll be able to go into combat— mentally, however, not so much. But he didn't have much of an option; they were going to send him out into the field sooner or later. He couldn't put it off for much longer.

"I can fight." He said more in an effort to convince himself rather than answer her question.

"That's good to hear. Tell me Corporal, how long do you plan on holding onto Private Nessler's chip?"

He was startled at the question, unsure of how to respond.

"I'm not sure what you're referring to…" he let the silence take over.

"Corporal, I know of your educational history. I'm also well aware of how Nessler's arm was delivered. The chip was removed while she was still alive. The doctors could attest to that."

"That doesn't mean I have it."

"There's no need to get defensive. Like I said earlier; doctor-patient confidentiality."

"I still don't know what you're talking about doc"

"Every time we discuss that day in Alaska, the day you almost died. The day she *did* die. You reach into your pocket. Any mention of her name or your past student career, you lift your hand and put it in your pocket and begin to fumble with something small. I notice these things, even when patients don't. It's a habit of yours, one you don't realize you're actively pursuing—a subconscious action."

He realized in that moment that he was in fact holding onto the chip. *How obvious could I be?* He wondered.

"Yes, I have her chip." There was no point in playing ignorance any more.

"Why?"

"A number of reasons…" he began. "It reminds me of her. Something of Alex's that I can hold on to. It's all we really have left of her…"

"Yes, anything else?"

"I wanted to learn more, to play around with the wiring, the coding behind it. I wanted to better understand how the chip works…It's inside my wrist as well. I just wanted to understand."

"That's all Corporal?"

"Yes, that's all. I'm not a threat. I can tell you that it is possible to re-activate a chip and reset it. I was able to breach certain levels of security…not much but enough for it to be a concern if anyone gets their hands on another chip."

"Corporal, we need to report this to the Sergeant."

"I understand."

Chapter 3

He continued on with his daily routine. Next stop—dormitory seven, the new arrivals' sector. Upon entering the room he didn't see anything obvious out of the ordinary. The beds were left unmade, a little unusual for soldiers but he shrugged it off.

Thinking back to what Bryans had said, he wondered if there was something there the three were hiding. As he changed the sheets, wiped off the floors, he quickly glanced at their bags. They had the same standard issue baggage given to most of the soldiers, soiled from the field and combat. Nothing strange there from an initial glance. As he got closer, he noticed that the baggage was part of the latest issue, a redesign meant for better weapon handling and convenience.

The side pockets, in the earlier models were meant merely for hydration purposes. The new models, met the demand of weapon transport. Bullets were to be safely stowed, while maintaining an ease of use when necessary to reload. Newly deployed soldiers were given the choice of three carry-on weapons. At least one of which was to be carried on their backs. Additional gun holders were sewn into the bags, meant for wrap-around purposes.

Those specific bags did not exist until just a couple years ago. If the new arrivals had been in combat for as long as they claimed, they'd have the prior version of the bag. There was no way they'd have been issued the new gear without having been to any of the barracks. He would have to tell Brinks and the Sergeant.

As he exited the dormitory, he quickly made his way to the Sergeant's office. He hesitated before entering, unsure of how to bring it up. He knew he should share the information, but he didn't want to come off as a rat.

"You can't ignore it Sergeant!" he heard Bryans screaming.

The Sergeant was calm, his voice muffled, Griffin couldn't quite make out exactly what he was saying.

"I'm backing him up on this one" Lynns' voice shot through.

He had to tell them, they were wasting time arguing. Instead, he waited and listened.

"Get out of my office, both of you. If there was a threat to security I'd have known about it. Theories are just that, theories. I will not have the two of you attacking innocent men—men, who have risked their lives just the same as you." The Sergeant was no longer in control, as the conversation took on a more emotional note.

The door swung open as Lynns stormed out, barely glancing in Griffin's direction. Bryans was still in with the Sergeant, continuing to argue his case, sounding more and more paranoid as he went on.

With the door ajar, this was his chance to speak up. He may not have another, if Bryans was gone, there'd be no one to back him up. They'd both sound insane.

Crouching by the doorway he saw the resident psychiatrist standing alongside Bryans, a look of concern sprawled across her face as thin fingers clutched at the notepad she had pressed against her chest. Commander Brinks stood by her side.

"You believe him?" The Sergeant looked towards the two.

"Yes, there's some viability there sir" Dr. Lorens said.

"Sir, you need to understand…if they reprogrammed those chips…" Bryans began.

"—enough! Have you accused them to their faces?"

"No sir"

"Who else have you raved your theories to?"

"No one sir…except…"

"Who? Except who?"

"Griffin Scoarse" he looked at the Doctor for confirmation.

"Scoarse?" Brinks finally spoke in confusion.

Upon hearing the mention of his name, Griffin quickly began moving away from the door to avoid being seen.

"You tell the staff of your theories without any evidence? Without any proof to back up your paranoia?" The Sergeant continued.

"I'm sorry sir but—"

"Get me Scoarse. NOW"

That was his cue as he shuffled away as fast as he could; knowing Bryans and Brinks would be out looking for him. This was not the time to tell the Sergeant of what he'd found. He reasoned it would only anger him further.

Picking up the laundry cart he'd left abandoned minutes prior, Griffin returned to his duties. Hauling up inside one of the dormitories he knew Bryans shouldn't have access to and Brinks wouldn't bother checking.

He'd only just begun to strip the bed sheets off the cots before he heard the familiar beeping sound of a door being activated. Looking up, he was surprised to see one of the new arrivals staring down at him.

Chapter 4

She gave up her life for nothing Lynns thought to himself as he swung open the door to his dormitory, almost damaging the wall behind it. He stormed over to his cot and quickly began packing away all of his gear and belongings.

"Those morons!" he screamed unable to control himself. He knew Bryans was on to something, treating the Corporal like a paranoid freak was too much for him. At this point, they deserve what they're going to get.

There was no way in hell he was going to stick around and wait for the place to collapse. Alex had given up her life for them; he wasn't going to waste it on the Sergeant's politics. Ignorance in this case, will lead to death; he wasn't about to let that happen.

He knew he could have reasoned better with the Sergeant, it had been wrong to let his emotions get the best of him. But for the present moment, there was nothing left to talk about. *They wanted hard proof, wasn't Bryans' ability to reprogram the chip on his own proof enough? Or the fresh wounds on each of the wrists of the "soldiers?"* Anger overtook whatever logic the Sergeant had, and his lackey of a Commander, Brinks, had his nose so far up his ass Lynns knew he was useless.

He frantically continued to throw everything he had into his duffel bag. He would need to get his hands on a few weapons before leaving, if they weren't going to release him for deployment. Stowing away his clothes and canteen, Lynns paused for a second.

He stared straight ahead, focusing on nothing but what was going on inside his head. He couldn't leave Bryans. He had enough proof to convince himself that staying at the barracks would result in a signed death certificate.

This was not the time to continue arguing, he needed to get out. But first, he had to find Bryans.

Packing up both his and the Corporal's belongings, he quickly walked back to the main hall. The new arrivals had already been here for twenty-four hours, whatever they were planning, he was certain it would happen soon.

As he ran through the hall, he practically bumped into Bryans as he turned the corner.

"We need to talk, now." He motioned towards their dorm.

"I can't, I need to find Scoarse. Sergeant's orders."

"Fuck the Sergeant. This is important." Again he gave way to his emotions.

"I have to find Scoarse." Bryans was stubborn, focused.

Pulling on his arm, Lynns directed him towards the room. "You can look for him on the way."

"Private, this is insubordination. We cannot disobey a direct order. No matter how miniscule you think it is." Yes, Bryans was definitely not losing his mind.

"Please...five minutes, I just need five minutes." Lynns graveled.

"You can speak while I search for Scoarse."

"This isn't that kind of conversation, we need privacy. If anyone hears..."

"Private, if it is important it shouldn't matter who hears."

"Stop talking to me by rank! We're friends, or have you forgotten *Corporal*?"

"Speak or don't. It's up to you." Bryans said as they turned towards the dormitories.

"Fine, about the new arrivals, you're right."

"Yes?" Bryans asked as pulled Alex's chip from his pocket.

"I mean, I trust you, your judgment. I don't have any evidence, just your word. But I trust you."

Bryans quickly opened one of the doors and peered in; disappointed he closed the door and moved on to the next.

"Where is this going Private?" he disarmed another lock.

"What we discussed before…"

"That would be abandonment, we cannot do that."

"Do they know about Alex's chip?"

"Yes, the doc knows. What I did, its treason. I need to find Scoarse and evidence before they hang me for my crimes."

"This is why we need to carry out our initial plans. If the Sergeant finds out about you having tampered with Alex's chip, breaking security protocol, which by the way, you're doing this very moment…"

"Then what Private? We just discussed this, I need to focus"

"Jason! We need to leave!"

"Keep your voice down Private."

Chapter 5

"You shouldn't have access to this room" Griffin went on, unsure of how to handle the situation.

"This is my room." Private Hash, the shortest of the three new arrivals stated. He revealed no expression as he spoke, almost robotic, as if it had been rehearsed.

"I'm sorry Private but there must be some mistake. This room was recently emptied; the occupants had been deployed this morning."

"There is no mistake. I was assigned this room this morning. Please leave now."

Griffin was taken aback; the guy had absolutely no personality. If the room assignments had been updated he should've been notified of the change. He needed to speak with the Sergeant after all.

He walked over towards the exit without saying a word. Looking down at his feet as he left the room he heard Bryans and Lynns approaching from the right.

"There you are! The Sergeant needs to see you." Bryans ran up to him.

Grabbing his elbow, Bryans directed him towards the main hall.

"About what?"

"The new men who've arrived, the ones I spoke to you about."

"What does he need to see me about that?" He wasn't sure if he should tell the Sergeant everything he knows. The last thing he needed was to piss the Sergeant off any further.

"I'm not entirely sure. Maybe to clarify on what we had discussed earlier."

The door to the Sergeant's office was wide open. The doctor had already left to her next appointment. Sergeant Benson was sitting by his desk, both hands cupping his head. *Something's off* Griffin thought to himself.

Bryans quietly knocked to let their presence be known as Lynns hurried away towards the dorms. After several seconds Benson still hadn't looked up. "Sergeant? Scoarse is here."

Still, no response. "Maybe we should come back another time Corporal…"

"Sergeant?" Bryans asked again.

"He doesn't want to discuss this, we should come back another time" Griffin whispered as Bryans slowly walked in towards the desk.

"He's not moving—"

"What?"

"He's not moving, he's not acknowledging our presence, Scoarse, we need to get help…"

Coming closer, Griffin didn't recognize the man sitting in the chair. "That's not the Sergeant. Look, it's just another soldier. He's wearing the Sergeant's clothes, someone staged this."

The collar was soaked red, blood seeping out from his throat, slowly dripping onto the hard floor below. Quiet drips, thumping down rhythmically.

"Then, where's Sergeant Benson?"

"Right here Bryans" the Sergeant said as he walked into the room. "You need to read this."

Chapter 6

A total of seventeen barracks across the country have been under attack. An unknown rebel group, leaving hundreds of thousands of soldiers dead, managed to breach security after countless of failed attempts prior. Please proceed with the mandatory security protocol for code D. Do not raise suspicion and maintain orderly operations in doing so.

The letter was sent out to all the remaining barracks within the country, a warning that they could be next.

Minimal information has been gathered due to the situation in which these attacks are being carried out. Central mainframe systems are now in reboot mode. Several glitches have been found and maintenance procedures are being carried out. The chip system will be upgraded to follow with the processes laid out in Code D.

As Bryans continued to read, Benson quietly shut the door.

"This does not leave this room, is that understand?" he said pointing to the dead soldier collapsed over his desk.

"There will be a lockdown tonight; no one is to leave their sleeping quarters past 22" he stated.

"Yes sir" Bryans and Griffin said simultaneously.

"I acknowledge that I may have chosen the wrong course of action when you first came to me with your suspicions Corporal."

"That's alright sir."

"No Corporal, we may have a security breach of our own. However, I'm still not entirely certain that the new arrivals are the rebels mentioned. I still require further proof."

"But Sir—"

"Corporal, I do apologize, but I have already killed one man in an attempt to maintain order. I will not take any more innocent lives unless I am certain that we absolutely have to."

"I do not mean to go against your command Sergeant, but I believe it wise to take them into custody. Keep them contained, as an additional safety precaution."

"I cannot raise suspicion Corporal."

"I may have some proof.." Griffin quietly piped up.

As if noticing him for the first time, the two simply stared and waited. After several seconds of hesitation Griffin continued.

"One of the men, I think his name was Hash, he entered into one of the dormitories that was part of my rounds for the day..." he paused, unsure of how to go on.

"Go on Scoarse" the Sergeant insisted.

"He claimed that it was his new assignment, his new room. But there were no updates on the sleeping arrangements sheet."

"You are certain that it was simply not a mistake?"

"Yes sir"

"They have access to the areas that should otherwise be secure, Sergeant they need to be detained—" Bryans went on.

Ignoring him the Sergeant remained focused on Griffin.

"Anything else?"

"Sergeant, I was doing my daily rounds, there's something else not right with them."

"And what's that Scoarse? Need I remind you, you are only a member of the staff, it is not your place to pass judgment on these men."

"I'm not judging, there are no assumptions, only an observation..." he paused, expecting to be silenced and rushed out. When neither occurred he went on, noticing that Bryans was now giving him his full attention. "Well one other thing, I thought was odd. I wasn't snooping, I just happened to notice their gear."

"What about their gear?"

"The standard issue bags. When were the most recent prototypes released to the soldiers?"

"The first round occurred only a little over two years ago, what's your point Scoarse?"

"If these men really are who they claim to be, they would possess the earlier gear. They would not have been able to get their hands on the new baggage."

"Yes, they've been in combat for almost a decade now..."

"If that were true Sergeant...then why do they have gear from the new issue currently in their possession?"

"I will need to see that for myself."

Chapter 7

"The room is empty Scoarse"

"Their bags were here, earlier this morning…"

"Is this, in fact, their room?"

"Yes, sir, I believe it was"

"You believe?"

"Yes"

"Listen Scoarse, this is a serious matter. There is an apparent threat to security and what very well be falsified accusations flying around. Do you have any real proof or not?"

"Sergeant—" Bryans began.

"Not now Corporal. Scoarse, what do you propose I do next? You have no proof. The both of you have apparently wasted my time on this little egg hunt of yours."

"Sergeant, the arrangements sheet, we can check the assigned rooms there. If there was a mistake we would know then." Bryans offered.

"Scoarse get me the updated dorm roster now"

"Yes sir" Griffin said as he quickly left the room. He knew he hadn't made a mistake, something was wrong. The roster will show that.

He made his way towards the nurses' hall to collect the list. Grabbing a copy off the bulletin he rushed back to the Sergeant without a single glance.

Looking down at his feet, he handed over the roster to Benson.

"Scoarse, I will ask again, are you certain this was their room?"

"Yes sir"

"So either you're lying or just confused."

"Excuse me sir?"

"This is not the room they are assigned to. Why don't you have a look" Benson stated as he handed back the roster.

There in the column of room assignments, were their names, all three; Greenburg, Hash, and Ticker. All assigned to the room he found Hash in earlier that day.

"What room is that Scoarse?"

"Dorm number 47G" he said without making eye contact. He could feel his ears burning red, sweat slowly dripping down his back. His clothes suddenly felt too tight, constricting.

"Right, is that the room you saw Hash in?"

"Yes sir"

"Could you have made a mistake?"

"I suppose so…"

"You suppose? You just accused these men of criminal felonies—of being terrorists, threats to national security, and that's all you could say?"

"I'm sorry sir but—"

"No, you two are right. Something is strange here."

"Sergeant?" Bryans asked confused.

"Someone is lying here, and by all accounts all signs point to the two of you. Scoarse return to my office now and wait for me there, I'll deal with you soon enough. As for you Corporal, this is treason."

"No Sergeant, you have to listen!" Bryans panicked as his fingers grasped the chip in his right pocket.

"I'm done listening to this crazy runaround. Where's your partner?"

" Private Lynns?"

"Yes, he's your last hope here."

They made their way to Bryans' dormitory. Noticing the room was left open, Bryans' heart dropped. *This won't look good.*

Chapter 8

"Explain NOW" Benson ordered.

"Sergeant, I have no idea…I don't know" Bryans knew Lynns would run. *Why did he pack my shit too?*

"Planning to leave? "

"No Sergeant, I didn't—"

"You didn't what? From what I'm seeing your gear is all packed and a Private under your command is nowhere to be found."

"Sergeant I didn't pack, I don't know where Private Lynns is. Whatever he did, it was not under my orders."

"Another scapegoat?"

"Sir you need to understand—"

"All I understand is what I see. And what I see isn't looking good for you Corporal. Your gear is packed and your man is gone."

"Sergeant Benson, I know how this looks. But I'm on your side, please listen to me. There's a serious security threat to the barracks, none of us are safe."

"Yes, I agree. There is a threat. You're being detained Corporal."

"Detained?"

"Yes. Glad you heard me correctly. This, by all accounts is treason." Benson said as he cuffed Bryans' hands behind his back and led him out to the hall.

"You will be kept in solitary and under heavy guard while I figure out what the hell we're going to do with you. You have a lot of questions to answer Corporal." He threw him into a small four by four room with no windows, a room resembling a prison cell more than anything else. Closing the door behind him, all the lights went out leaving Bryans alone with his own thoughts and Alex's forgotten chip.

****

Griffin waited patiently for the Sergeant's return. His palms were sweating and his collar a little too close to his throat. He could hear Bryan's screaming from several feet away before a heavy door was shut and the all too familiar beep of a lock mechanism taking over.

****

"Is everything set in place?" Ticker asked of the other two.

"Yes Tim, everything is ready to go." Greenburg responded.

"The lockdown won't affect us. I overheard them talking earlier, everyone is to be locked in their rooms at ten pm." Hash explained.

"What time is it now?" Ticker asked.

"Five minutes to ten." Hash replied.

"Perfect" Ticker smiled.

****

"What are we going to do with you, Scoarse?" Benson asked as he stepped inside his office.

"Sergeant, it was my mistake. I read the rooms wrong."

"We've verified that already. You see, either you were in on it or you're easily influenced."

"When he told me about his suspicions, I let that cloud my judgment…"

"So, you're a coward as well as an idiot?"

"Yes sir" Griffin acknowledged with his head bent down.

"You see that dead soldier in my seat?"

Griffin slowly nodded.

"Walk over to him, lift him off the chair and place him onto the floor."

Griffin did as he was told, careful not to get any of the blood on himself.

"Now, take the seat Scoarse" Benson ordered.

"Sir?" he asked confused.

"Take the fucking—" before he finished his sentence, the hall behind him shook as a deafening thud rang through their ears.

Looking up, Griffin found the Sergeant's face, burnt entirely off.

He got up and headed out the door. Before making it halfway down the hall another explosion went off leaving him face down on the cold linoleum floor.

****

He felt the ground shake from under him. Getting up, Bryans slowly walked towards the small opening in the shut door. He could see the fire, the smoke, the dead trying to run from their already dug graves.

He quickly pulled Alex's chip out, the small red light was still blinking, still had some life in it. Pulling it closer to the lock he heard the cringe of disarmed locks as his door slowly swung open. *I need to get them out.*

Running from the room he headed towards the dorms, right

into the blackened fog. Men were crawling, crying all around him. He continued to push through. *I need to stop them.*

Barely making it more than ten steps into the hall, a third explosion rocked him, nocking him to the ground. He could feel the burning sting of his flesh, forcing himself not to look down at his legs. His own screams now lost in the harmony of all the others.

Chapter 9

There was smoke everywhere, screaming soldiers falling amongst the debris as another explosion went off.

"Griffin, you need to get up." He looked up to find Alex's face; behind her the bright orange sear continued to envelope the hall.

"Alex? I'm scared…"

"We're all scared…we get to that point where we realize we're not that special after all, we're just like every other microscopic bobble head out there. We have to work, be responsible; commit…there's nothing more frightening than realizing that you're just like everybody else. And then, and only then, do we reevaluate ourselves, challenge our beliefs, let go of the foundation, change ourselves. Take risks to stand out. And the most you can hope for is that those risks pay off."

"Alex?" they were in his backyard. The sun was out, the clouds slowly moving overhead, sipping calmly on their ice-cold beers.

"Griffin, you need to get up and do something, *really* do something…" it was the last conversation they were going to have before the relationship would end.

Looking up at her, her surroundings quickly began to change. She was still speaking but he couldn't hear a word, only see her lips moving as those around them ran and burned. Her flesh was starting to sear, burn as she spoke, her words becoming nothing more than ash.

And just like that, she was gone.

He tried to get up, forcing his body straight as his head

spun around. Through the disorienting fog, he saw his mother. "Griffin, when are you going to get up?" her voice was steady, but he knew she was upset. Standing there by his bedroom door she smiled disapprovingly down at him still lying in bed. "It's already noon, you need to get up."

She was still pretty, even in her forties. Always nurturing towards him, protective.

"I'm leaving for work Griffin, you need to get up" she said as her smile began to melt away, her face dripping to the floor replaced by debris and blood.

The smell of burnt flesh was everywhere, ash flying all around him as he tried desperately to make sense of his surroundings. There were dozens of others all around him. Limbs left without owners, screams deafened by smog, and faces blurred by the chaos.

Further down he spotted her familiar blonde hair. Gold shining through from the grey and red. Waves like his mother's and eyes of his past best friend. There she was, burning with the rest of them. Her skin blackening, charring as the seconds ticked by. He tried to get to her, to crawl towards her as he steadied himself against the wall.

She was fading away; he tried desperately to pick up his speed. His leg holding him back, his lungs filling up with smoke. Surrounded by the dead, he tried not to trip over their lost flesh and bones.

He blinked away the smoke, regaining his focus on her. But, she was gone. All he saw was just another pile of ash. *It couldn't have been her.* He reasoned as he made his way towards the nearest exit. Ignoring all the others, pretending their cries didn't matter, he only focused on his own survival.

He needed to get home, needed to get back to her.

"Help me" he looked down to find a half dead soldier, part

of his face charred off, pulling down on his ankle. "Scoarse help me"

Kicking him off he continued towards the exit, he needed the fresh air. He couldn't help anyone if he wasn't able to help himself first.

Bryans laid there, caressing Alex's chip as he watched Griffin peel away from him. He couldn't feel the lower half of his body, scared to look down and see the damage. He should've ran with Lynns. *Heroes don't survive in this world anymore* he thought as he watched Griffin get farther and farther away, *only cowards do.*

Chapter 10

He covered his nose and mouth with the sleeve of his shirt as he ran past the injured men. All of the exits were on lockdown by now, triggered by the Sergeant's earlier request. He remembered the door in the back of the kitchen, an emergency exit kept for safety protocol in case of fire. Pushing through the steel swinging doors he briskly moved towards the one exit he knew would be open, ignoring all the men behind him.

The handle was hot from the heat of the explosions. Flinching from the searing pain he instinctively jerked his hands away from the exit. Looking back, he could see Brinks making his way towards him. The Commander was about seven feet away, crawling as best he could towards the exit. *He won't make it.* Griffin thought to himself as he once more pushed down at the handle, this time with the right side of his entire body, careful not to make direct contact with the burning metal.

The lights surrounding the barracks were blinding. He barely made it through the exit as another explosion went off.

Walking out, he heard the door slam shut behind him, encasing the fire inside.

Making it out he forced his way towards the direction of the train. Right outside the barracks he could see the building filling up with smoke, consumed by bright red. The commotion outside, other civilians those trying to help, only made him more weak. He pushed through searching for fresher, calmer air.

As he tried to make his way out, he could feel the air filling up in his lungs, making him dizzy as he moved alongside the wall of the building. Within seconds a frenzied crowded surrounded him, yelling at him, asking if he was all right.

He looked up at the blurred muddle of concerned citizens before collapsing onto the ground.

****

"Sir, can you tell me your name?"

He was still groggy as he attempted to open his eyes. The bright lights overhead forced them back closed.

"Sir, do you know where you are?"

Slowly, he lifted his lids. Someone with a clipboard in a white jacket was standing over him, a doctor it seemed, or maybe a nurse.

"Sir?" she asked. "Sir, can you tell me your name?"

"Grif... Griffin Scoarse" he managed to gargle from his throat.

"Mr. Scoarse you are in the Presbyterian Hospital. You were admitted here after the attack on the Barracks. Do you remember the attack?"

"Yes" he mumbled, becoming more aware of his surroundings.

"You've been admitted due to high levels of smoke inhalation. You may feel a tightness in your chest when taking deep breaths, but you'll be okay." The nurse smiled at him.

"Where... are there others?"

She looked down bleakly. "I'm sorry Mr. Scoarse, no other survivors have been found yet. You need to rest. You'll have a few visitors admitted to see you shortly, regain your strength in the meantime."

He nodded as he closed his eyes. *Visitors? I knew she'd come..* he thought before he fell asleep again.

After just minutes he heard a knock at the door. Opening his eyes he was both surprised and disappointed to see military men approach him.

"Good evening Mr. Scoarse, I'm General Wyatt. How are you feeling?"

"Better" he said as he steadied himself to an upright position.

"Glad to hear it. We have a few brief questions we'd like your help on, and then we'll leave you to it. We spoke to your doctor, Dr. Rechter, we've been given the green light."

Griffin nodded.

"Mr. Scoarse we understand you survived the attack on the Barracks in the Northeast sector?"

"Yes sir"

"Are you aware of how this attack took place?"

"I'm not sure.." he hesitated. Unsure of what he should say.

"Anything you're able to tell us, any details at all, would really help us out here."

"I understand. There were three soldiers, recent arrivals. From Alaska I believe...they had decoded the access chips. That's all I know..."

"Thank you. Are you able to tell us why no bodies were

found in the left wing of the Barracks? Why everyone appeared to be in the exact same area?"

"The Sergeant, he requested a lock down. All men were to be in their dorms."

"Why was this request made?"

"He received a letter. It informed him to do so. There were other attacks."

"Interesting. Thank you Mr. Scoarse."

"Wait!" Griffin called after them as they made their way out.

"Yes?"

"Were there other attacks…besides us?"

"No Mr. Scoarse, there weren't…not yet at least. Again, thank you for your time."

Epilogue

He was released twenty-four hours later with nothing but the burned clothes he'd been admitted in. He checked his pockets for his belongings and found that everything was still in place, including a small metal chip, the red light dimly blinking. He quickly grabbed for a cigarette and lit it, ignoring the dull pain in his chest as he did so.

Making his way back, he found that the trains were stalled. Nothing was moving. The city was at a standstill. He had to make it back to her. Walking was his only option.

The further he got, the cooler the air became. After several hours he needed to rest. Picking a lonely bench overlooking the hills across the bridge, he finally sat down.

Looking around at all the houses, built on top of the once natural land, he thought of his life, his survival. Trees and forestation had been cleared out decades ago to make room for the now empty streets and abandoned homes. Houses once filled with light, and warmth were now left unoccupied but for the possessions that had been left behind so long ago, proof that there was once life, now replaced by ghosts. Possessions that had seemed so valuable just a lifetime ago, now obsolete, worthless, relics of what used to be.

The bricks and wood, the buildings and concrete, were slowly giving way to the earth that consumes it. Hiding the architecture, replacing it with new shrubbery, disarrayed weeds. Soon enough, any proof humanity will cease to exist. Hidden by what we destroyed.

He got up once again, his limbs upset with him for doing

so. Making his way towards the nearest station, he heard a rumble, an engine come to life, the trains had finally resumed.

He entered his small apartment, relieved to finally be back. Not giving a second thought to the destruction and death he left behind only hours prior.

The apartment was as he'd left it. Dark, cluttered, and lonely. Turning the lights on inside his closet of a kitchen he called for her.

"Becks? You must've heard what happened..." he walked towards his bedroom, assured that she was there.

"Becks?" he called out again after not hearing a response.

His bedroom was empty—the apartment was empty. She wasn't there. He searched for her familiar scent, but couldn't grasp it. He went to the living room, but there was no sign.

No articles of clothing, no additional used glassware, not even a single gold strand; she wasn't there.

"Becks?" he called out once more, reserving hope that she was still there, anywhere.

He lit up again, thinking back to her. Wondering why she hadn't made an attempt to see him at the hospital. There was no sign of her; it was as if she never existed.

He sat back onto his old, brown, springy couch, listening and hearing nothing but his own steady breathing as he inhaled the cigarette. The recollection of her last words to him slowly repeated themselves from inside his head; *and when it's all over will you be able to remember how it all began? Or is the beginning the one thing that'll remain clear and the events in between suddenly blur into nothing?...Let's just pretend that nothing and everything exist all at the same time.*

Slowly he let go and let his exhaustion consume him, his eyelids finally closing. Only to reopen to the glaring red of the sun shining through his curtain, the same as it always had.

CPSIA information can be obtained at www.ICGtesting.com
Printed in the USA
BVOW08s0046211115

428001BV00001B/8/P